Just My
Imagination

Narell I. Hunt

ISBN – 978-1-7352351-4-1 (Paperback)
ISBN – 978-1-7352351-0-3 (E-book)

Just my Imagination is a fictional novel. Names, characters, places, and occurrences were created using the author's imagination. Any use of name of persons within novel, dead or alive is completely coincidental.

Editing by Joshua Price
Front Cover Image by DuDess & DuDe
Book Design by Daiana Marchesi & Saqib Arshad
Ebook Design by Mohamed Hussam

LilacSky, LLC
Narell I. Hunt
4550 Jonesboro Road Ste A2 #322
Union City, GA 30291 United States
Lilacskyllc@gmail.com

LILACSKY BOOKS
JUST MY IMAGINATION

Narell I. Hunt lives in Georgia with her daughter; however, was born and raised in New York City. She is a college graduate who majored in Paralegal studies, but found her passion with her first love, creative writing.

Special thanks and praises to the Most High God, and to friends and family who encouraged me along the way.

To:

Nia

Everything is connected, though we may not see, that our lives are a testament, to help others during their own journey.

-Narell I. Hunt

CONTENTS

MOTHER EARTH

MOTHER EARTH

***

Earth longed to give life. Unfortunately, her circumstances left her unable to produce. Having to accept her fate was difficult and left Earth with a feeling of bitterness that made her heart cold. She would often snap at her closest friends, resulting in her being alone—becoming isolated. As Earth was resting, she dreamed of different colors, objects, and hues of green, blue, gold, red, and purple. Earth abruptly awoke. She stood panicking, heart racing; Earth had not ever seen such shades. They felt so real to her, made her feel gratitude. Her heart began to change.

Earth began missing her family and decided to make amends with her sister, Venus. "My actions and words have been unkind, and I apologize. Can you forgive me?"

Venus looked at her with forgiveness already written on her face. "Yes. I already have."

"How do you do that?" asked Earth.

"Do what?" Venus replied.

"Be as forgiving as you are—even after you've been wronged? Beautiful beings must have it easy," Earth said, cracking a smile.

Venus laughed. "Look who's talking," she shot back. The two laughed, bringing joy back into their sisterhood.

"My secret is something called love. Showing love is not only for the outer beings, but for your inner being as well. Love is the only thing you truly must give—don't you remember our teachings? Think about it."

Earth took her sister's advice; though it took much time and patience, she eventually mastered the art of responding with love instead of anger. Earth began to understand the inner happiness her sister spoke of, and laughter began singing from Earth's soul. Word began to travel about Earth, and the change that she made, and the cause of it, but some had difficulty believing that a dream is what caused her to make a change; and if she truly had changed at all.

"It's just a dream," some would say. These words made Earth question herself, and she almost talked herself into believing that it was "just a dream," and although Venus encouraged Earth to keep going, she was growing weary of talking about it herself. Earth continued to believe that one day, her dream would come to fruition, instead of resulting back to anger as she did before.

One day, while Earth was ruminating on the dream, she noticed something in the far distance coming towards her. She glanced at her sister to see if she saw it as well, and she did. *Closer and closer- heading* in their direction. *"It can't be,"* Earth thought, *"is that light?!"* The light shined so brightly over Earth that it pushed back the darkness, and Earth smiled with glee as the light covered her like a blanket, giving her warmth and comfort.

Suddenly, Earth began to transform, and within days, she had green grass, a beautiful blue sky, animals, and even the object from her dream; its name was man. How happy Earth became seeing that with the power of love, she was able to attract the light needed for her to produce *life*. With the start of a dream, Earth could finally say that she had been given the title—*mother*!

SARAI,
REDDINGTON
And The
CARDINAL

SARAI, REDDINGTON, AND THE CARDINAL

———————— ⟩ᘒᘒᘖ ————————

Sarai was born to a scorned woman left alone to raise her. When Sarai learned to tie her shoes, her mother was not impressed. When Sarai drew pictures, Sarai's mother gave them a glance and condemned the colors she chose. When Sarai sang a tune, her mother laughed and told her to stop trying. Sarai yearned for acceptance from her mother, but instead, was shunned. Sarai often sat alone in a corner, hoping her mother would one day want her—maybe even notice her.

One morning, Sarai was awakened by the singing of birds coming from outside her window. Sarai looked out and noticed two beautiful red cardinals chirping and hopping from branch to branch. Amazed at their beauty, Sarai opened her window to allow the singing to fill her room.

Suddenly, one bird flew towards Sarai and landed on the ledge of her window and said, "What is your name?"

Sarai's eyes opened wide, and with a tone of uncertainty, she asked, "Did you just speak to me?"

She jumped back as the cardinal hopped closer. "Yes, don't be frightened. My name is Reddington. What is your name?"

"My name is Sarai," she said softly.

"Nice to meet you, Sarai. Would you like to come with us?"

Sarai looked around her cold, dark room and said, "Yes."

She grabbed her blanket and quietly sneaked out the back door to follow Reddington and the other cardinal. They accompanied Sarai, and all three sang a tune. The birds led Sarai deep into the forest. As night began to fall, she grew frightened, and, noticing Sarai becoming fearful, Reddington assured her that they were close and not to be scared. Moments later, they stopped at a very tall and large tree.

"Wait here," Reddington told Sarai.

The birds flew up the length of the tree, leaving Sarai on the ground alone. She leaned against the tree and sat down beside it. She hugged her legs towards her body and put her head down.

Suddenly, the tree began to shake, and the ground began to rumble. The cardinals came flying down, and Sarai got up to await their next direction. As the rumbling continued, Sarai turned her attention to the tree trunk, and out of nowhere, a door appeared. Reddington motioned for the door with his wing. "Don't worry—we'll go in with you. Open it."

Sarai hesitantly grabbed the latch and pulled open the door. She looked inside, and to her surprise, she saw children playing, an abundance of trees, grass, wildflowers, birds of all kinds, and butterflies of all colors. Sarai ran inside, and the birds followed.

"What is this place?!" Sarai asked with excitement.

"A place for children like you," said Reddington.

VONDA

VONDA

Tending to her roses kept her sane. Vonda, once again, found herself in a daze. She occasionally drifted off in deep thought when staring at objects, and today, Vonda found herself immersed in a red rose. For many people, their gardens consisted of a variety of vegetation, but not Vonda. Her garden consisted only of roses—pinks, yellows, reds, and whites. A beauty to all who saw.

There was a knock at the door. Vonda snapped out of her trance and went to see who it was. It was Donnie. He worked at the grocery store in the city. She had met him while she was shopping one day when he helped her bring her groceries to her car. Noticing her beauty and her discomfort for the outside, he introduced himself and asked if she wanted to sign up for home delivery. She agreed, and he had been making deliveries to her house ever since.

Vonda took a deep breath, checked herself in the mirror, and slowly opened the door. Donnie stood smiling with his hands in his pockets before the door was even fully open. She smiled back, said hello, and started helping him inside with the groceries.

"How are you this morning, Vonda?" he asked

"I'm well, Sir Donnie."

"*Sir Donnie?*" Donnie looked at Vonda with confusion. "Why are you being so formal?"

Vonda let out a laugh. "I'm in the middle of writing, and my character is from the 1900s. So yes, she's very formal."

"I see. Is that what you were doing before I arrived, or were you tending to those roses?"

Vonda looked at Donnie, intrigued that he had guessed correctly. "Yes, as a matter of fact, I was."

"And when can I see this beautiful garden?"

"How'd you know it was beautiful?"

Donnie stopped putting the groceries into the refrigerator and said, "Because you are."

They share a warm stare.

"Thank you, Donnie. You are too kind. How about you get going—I can take it from here."

With a hint of disappointment in his voice, Donnie said, "Okay." He set the rest of the groceries on the kitchen island, and Vonda began to escort Donnie out. She thanked him again and closed the door.

After bringing her groceries, Donovan would often stay a little longer just to chat Vonda up. He did not like that she lived alone, so far from town. As Vonda was putting away her groceries, Missy rubbed her head and the rest of her body along Vonda's right leg.

"Someone's hungry. Come, my dear. Let us bring your bowl out into the garden. You can eat out here with me," Vonda said to Missy.

Vonda was a woman who had experienced much trauma, from a painful childhood to a brutal divorce, which had ultimately led to unhealthy relationships. She sought to be alone; she found comfort in it. It allowed her to not worry about the feeling of others, and if (or when) they would eventually hurt hers.

As Vonda got older, she became less talkative—until she met her ex-husband. He would talk to Vonda for hours. She admired how well he could express himself. He loved attention and had the art of captivating others with his many stories. Vonda did not mind it, just if she was on his arm. Vonda and her husband were the perfect match—until she began to excel at her career as an author.

Vonda's husband was not able to handle the fame and attention his wife was getting. Unlike Vonda, he did not like sharing the spotlight. Her fans would swarm her, leaving him waiting on the sidelines, which resulted in the couple growing apart. The morning he asked for a divorce, it was raining. She sat at the edge of the bed with her back opposite to him. He explained that they had grown apart, and it was time for them to go their separate ways. A teardrop fell as she listened to her husband's words. She stared out the window, watching the raindrops fall, letting the sound of the rain tune out his voice as he continued to complain about how unhappy he was.

After the divorce, Vonda continued to focus on her work, herself, and her ragdoll cat, Missy. A few years later, she met Donovan. At first glance, he was easy to look at, but there was no way a 49-year-old should have any dealings with a young man in his late 20s. She knew Donnie was attracted to her; after all, she looked half her age since she was a stickler for eating right and regular check-ups; "health is wealth" her adopted mother would say, but the chances of Donnie delivering more than groceries were slim to none. It was too difficult for her to take that next step with anyone.

A month passed, and it was time for Vonda to order her groceries. She thought about what she would say to Donnie when she saw him. *"Maybe I should have him stay for dinner,"* she thought. She prepared her order and waited for Donnie to arrive. Hours later, her bell rang.

Vonda fixed herself up and opened the door with haste. "Don—" She instantly swallowed the other half of the name and repeatedly blinked at the other person, thinking it was going to be Donovan who normally brings her delivery.

"Hello, ma'am, I'm Suzie. I am delivering your groceries. Where would you like me to place them?"

"Hello, Suzie. You can just set them down by the door—I'll bring them in." Vonda went into her bag and handed Suzie a one-hundred-dollar tip. "You deserve that after driving this far. Thank you."

Suzie lets out a smile from ear to ear, almost wanting to hug Vonda, but she kept her composure. "Thank you!" And she skipped back to her car.

MONTHS LATER

Vonda woke up to her cat beside her bed, meowing. She rose and headed to the kitchen. Vonda looked at the calendar on the refrigerator; it had a reminder on it. *"My Birthday"* She saw the notification, but it didn't instantly register. After taking a second for the notification to sink in, Vonda came to the realization herself.

"Not like I could do much anyway—except watch a few movies and get some writing done," Vonda thought to herself.

As she was preparing Missy's meal, the bell rang. Vonda stopped instantly and considered who it could be, and to her surprise, it was Donnie. Vonda couldn't stop staring at him through her drapes. It wasn't until Donnie rang the bell for the third time that she snapped out of it.

Vonda slowly opened the door and looked up at Donnie.

Before she could speak, he handed her a bouquet of red roses and said, "Happy birthday—may I come in?"

Still staring and now smiling, she said, "Yes." She tried to keep from smiling too hard. "How did you know it was my birthday?"

"Now, how could I be interested in a woman and not find out who she is? I saw on your Facebook page that you're an author, and I saw that you had a birthday coming up, so I decided to surprise you."

"I'm impressed."

"Well, I had to get to know you somehow since someone's always pushing me away. Maybe I can get to know you a bit better," said Donnie as he smiled at Vonda.

Continuing the conversation, Donnie added, "Are you happy that I'm here?"

"Yes. I am," Vonda responded, trying to refrain from smiling due to her cheeks beginning to ache.

"Would you be so kind as to give me your autograph? Donnie pulled Vonda's first novel, *Secrets from The Ruler*, from his back pocket and handed it to her.

"Sure," Vonda said while heading to her study for a pen. "Can I get you anything—a glass of wine maybe… water, tea?"

"I should be asking you that; it's your day. What do you have planned?"

"I don't have any plans. I'm a little embarrassed to admit this, but I actually forgot today was my birthday, so I just plan to write."

"I admire your dedication to your work; you are definitely a great writer, but wouldn't you like to take a break just for today, maybe paint the town red?"

"Eh, I just don't feel like being around people, Donnie; it's too much, I'd rather stay in."

"Okay, no pressure, but I'm not going to leave you alone on your day. May I stay in with you?"

Vonda looked up at Donnie, happy that he had asked. "Yes, you may."

They spent the evening with Donnie making dinner for the two, laughing, and watching "sappy" romantic movies—as Vonda would describe them, but she did not mind because this time, she wasn't watching them alone. Not paying attention, Vonda accidentally spilled wine on her blouse. She jumped up, holding her hands out, embarrassed by her clumsy mishap. Donnie headed to the kitchen to grab a rag.

He dampened it and handed it to Vonda while he cleaned the wine on the couch. "The key is to dab the spill with water. Then it will dry without staining."

"Who taught you that?" asked Vonda, looking at Donnie, impressed.

"My mother—she was a bit of neat freak."

"Were you close with your mother?" asked Vonda.

Without making eye contact, and still cleaning, Donnie solemnly said, "Not as close as I would have liked."

Vonda stopped, sensing the sadness in Donnie's tone, and touched his back. "I'm sorry, I know how that can be."

He gave Vonda a quick smile and brought the rag back into the kitchen.

"I didn't mean to reopen any wounds, Donnie, and I apologize if I did."

"No need to apologize. These wounds should've been healed."

Donnie took a step back to admire Vonda. "Can I do something for you without you becoming frightened?" he asked.

Vonda looked at Donnie with one eyebrow raised. "What?"

"Ah Ah! Just trust me and tell me which bathroom we can use."

Vonda led him to the bathroom in the guest bedroom.

Donnie looked inside. "Perfect." He took Vonda's hand and led her inside, set towels on the floor, and started running the bath.

Vonda stared at Donnie, confused. "What are you doing?"

Donnie did not say anything. He continued to run the bath while taking off his watch. He then took her hands and helped her to sit on the towels he laid out. He then took out her hair clip and began washing her hair. Vonda, without a fight, closed her eyes and enjoyed the moment; not even her ex-husband ever washed her hair. After several months, the pair became inseparable. Vonda and Donnie had found love.

PART II

I admire you and all of your accomplishments, Vonda, and I've been doing some thinking."

Vonda continues to pet Missy while she is laying on her lap. "I'm listening, dear." "Well, I'm thinking about joining the Air Force."

"The Air Force?!" Vonda stopped petting Missy and looked at Donnie with concern. "Why?"

"I love being with you, around you, talking to you, but there some things I have to do for me," he explained.

"Do for you?" Vonda repeated, hoping it would provide clarity to what Donnie was saying.

"I feel like I haven't accomplished anything, I feel like a nobody with a successful girlfriend who I want to make a wife, but I can't because I can only give half of myself."

"Half of himself?!" Vonda shouted, startling Missy.

Seeing that she was upset, Donnie walked over to console her. "Come here," he said while pulling her off the couch and close to him. "I'm doing this not only for me—but for us," he said calmly, hoping Vonda would understand.

Vonda wrapped her arms around him and said nothing but, "Hold me."

And he does. "I know this is sudden, but I need to find myself. You have your passion, but what do I have?" Vonda remained silent. He continued to explain himself in hopes of getting a response from his newfound love, but not a word was spoken from her lips.

16

With her head on his chest and his arms around her, she said, "What do you want for dinner?"

Donnie tried to make eye contact, but Vonda refused to take her head from his chest. "Dinner? Vonda, I am trying to have a conversation with you. What do you mean, 'What do I want for dinner?'"

Vonda picked her head up without responding. Instead, she said, "I'm thinking about Red Snapper. What do you think?"

Donnie was upset, but he understood that the topic was too much for Vonda, so he just said, "Okay. Red snapper it is."

THE NEXT MORNING

The home was chilly and quiet. At around 7am, Vonda woke up to feed Missy, and then she went into her study to do some yoga and meditation. She wanted to continue to brainstorm new story ideas but could not. She had Donnie on her mind. Vonda laid on her mat with her eyes closed, listening to the yoga instructor on YouTube. She was trying to focus on her breathing and the instructor, but Donnie's words continued to play in her mind like a broken record.

"*I need to find myself.*" Vonda took a deep breath in. "*What do I have?*" She exhaled. "*Half of myself.*" She took another deep breath and tried counting back from ten, but Donnie's voice and words did not seem to quiet themselves. She stopped the video and popped up from the mat, and then she headed to the guest bedroom where Donnie was sleeping.

She pulled up a chair and sat beside the bed to watch Donnie as he slept. She stared at him as he breathed, observing his chest moving up and down. She watched his eyes and considered what he was dreaming, and whether he was dreaming of her.

She grabbed her journal and began to write:

Dear Journal:

I love this man, and he wants to leave. I cannot have that. I do not want to hurt him, but him leaving me would be too much for me to bear. I do understand him wanting to find himself, but I cannot get over this nagging feeling that that is an excuse. He wants to leave me alone, like how everyone else has.

I just need time to think.

Father Ruler, I know you are not pleased with my behavior. Forgive me for my sins, and help me find a proper way to love, but I cannot cease this feeling of needing another love in my life aside from you. Please forgive me. Please forgive me. Please forgive me.

SINCERELY,

VONDA

Donnie began to come to, with Vonda lying next to him. He tried to put his arm around her, and—realizing his current circumstance—started to struggle with the cuffs.

"Vonda, can I at least brush my teeth?" he said, smiling at her.

Vonda laid her head on his shoulder. "How'd you sleep, baby?" she asked calmly.

"I mean, I slept okay—feel a bit sluggish, though, how many glasses of wine did we have?"

Vonda shrugs. "Don't recall, sugar plum; what are we having for breakfast?

"I thought I was having you, the way you have me cuffed." Donnie lets out a charming smile.

Vonda lets out a laugh. "Ha! You see, it is that sense of charm and humor you have. That is why I cannot just let you leave. I would miss it immensely."

Donnie began staring at Vonda, confused as to why she had not taken the cuffs off yet. "Vonnie, it's something I need to do for myself."

"NO!!!!" Vonda bellowed out.

Donnie's eyes widened. "Vonda, let me out of these cuffs, and let's talk about this."

"No, Donnie," Vonda said in a calmer tone. "I will not let you out of the cuffs, and can you please tell me what I should prepare for breakfast?"

"So, your idea is to hold me hostage, Vonda? Are you insane?! Let me out of these cuffs!"

"NO!! and do not raise your voice at me, Donovan."

Vonda pointed at Donnie's electric ankle monitor. "If you scream, or try anything—I will set this off, and it does not feel pretty, I can assure you."

Donnie lied back down and looked up at the ceiling. "Vonda, this is crazy. You're being crazy."

Vonda popped up and headed to the drawer for the remote. "CRA-ZY!!" she yelled, and then she set off the electric bracelet.

He clenched his teeth and breathed heavily. "Okay, okay—Vonda, take it easy."

She placed the remote back in the drawer, far away from his reach. "I understand that your mad, pumpkin. No one deserves to be drugged, handcuffed, and zapped, but I must make you understand that here is where you need to be. I am in love with you."

"Vonnie, I love you too, but this is not the way," Donnie pleaded.

Vonda kissed him on the forehead. "I'll be back."

Vonda turned on ESPN for Donnie, and then headed downstairs to prepare breakfast. As she walked out of the room, Missy jumped up on the bed next to Donovan.

Donnie looked over at Missy and made sure the door was closed before he whispered to the cat, "Your mom is crazy."

Donnie lay there cuffed and tagged, thinking of numerous ways to get out of the cuffs, but his determination was short-lived as his attention turned to the anchor that was going over stats from last night's game.

Days passed, and Vonda became ashamed of what she had done. Although Donovan was able to convince Vonda to take him out of the cuffs, she refused to remove the electric anklet. It happened that Donovan became angry that he pushed her down and tried to grab the remote from her robe she began to carry it in. He was not successful, and Vonda set the anklet off, causing Donnie to drop. Since that day, he complied and fell silent. He was not hurt for himself but for the woman he loved. She was sick, and there was not anything he could do to make her better.

He wanted to leave but was worried she would commit suicide. So, he stayed out of pity.

✳ ✳ ✳

"Are you going to leave me, Donnie. I thought you had when I didn't see you in the house." She said after finding him in the garden looking over at the rising sun.

Donnie continued to keep his focus on what he was looking at and said nothing.

Unable to take his silence much longer, Vonda continued,

"I didn't mean it. I just did not want you to leave. When I was younger, I was invisible. I was unwanted. I was abandoned. When I became married, I was only good for him in the meantime. Now he is off spending money that I worked for. Caught him cheating twice—and I stayed. But the moment he became uncomfortable with the attention I was receiving, married life became too much for him, and he wanted out. Not just out, he wanted out with an allowance. It's not even about the money, it's about him—"

"Abandoning you," Donnie said, finishing her sentence, still with his attention on the horizon.

"Yes," Vonda proclaimed. For the first time, she was opening herself to someone about trauma she kept hidden.

"When you first walked into the grocery store, 'How amazing,' I thought to myself. The light that shined with you. The smile that you carried. The way I followed you could have gotten me fired, but I couldn't help myself. I could tell that you were lonely, and I did not want you to feel that way any longer. Call me crazy, but I fell in love with you that day" He turns his attention to Vonda, and her eyes filled with water.

"You told me your name, and yes, I asked around town about you, and found out that you are a writer. My heart stopped. '*Beautiful and gifted,*' I thought; but what I did not think was that you're insane Vonnie. I genuinely love you, but I can't be with you if this is how you are when things aren't going your way."

Tears started flowing down Vonda's face hearing Donnie's words.

"When I was younger," Vonda started, "I dreamed of these red cardinals that took me to a magical place, a place just for me. I was there for days. The children and I drank from the river, ate the fruits from the tree—so many to choose from. I slept peacefully in my own treehouse, built just for me, and all the children would come to get me early mornings to run out and play."

Donnie looked on intensely.

"Imagine my surprise when I woke up in a hospital bed—covered in bandages, hooked up to a heart monitor." Vonda continued to explain, "The article read:

SEVEN-YEAR-OLD GIRL FOUND BEATEN NEARLY TO DEATH:

'Seven-year-old Sarai Airtafae was found in her mother's SUV one evening, as deputies pulled the suspect over for a minor traffic stop...'

One night, as I lay asleep, my mother came into my room with a metal baseball bat, and just started beating me. How does a woman go from not acknowledging your existence to just beating you? Beat me to the point of almost dying. She put me in the back of her trunk to toss my body, and because of a traffic stop by a state trooper, I was found. I imagine her hands were still bloody, gripping the steering wheel, her face in a daze. He made her pop the trunk, and there I was.

A woman and her husband adopted me. She became my mother, and he became my father. She asked if I wanted to keep my birth name, Sarai, but I said no. I wanted to forget Sarai, and she looked at me and said, 'How about Vonda? Though you are more beautiful than any Miss America.' That was the first time I was called beautiful." Vonda let out a short laugh and smiled, her tears still flowing.

"I'm sorry that you had to go through that, Vonnie. I could only imagine the pain you felt, but also, remember to be grateful that you were shielded by The Ruler. He protected you from the truth of what happened. He allowed you peace in a place beyond belief. You only knew about what happened to you because you read about it."

Vonda looked at Donnie surprised that he didn't diminish her dream as nothing more than just that. She took a key from her robe pocket and removed the anklet. "I'm sorry for what I've done to you, Donnie. Forgive me."

After that second shock, Donnie swore to himself that when Vonda released the anklet from him, that he was going to give her a good knock-out and head straight for the door.

But now that the opportunity had presented itself, he stood there and could only hug her.

GREEN EYED MONSTER

GREEN-EYED MONSTER

———————— ꙮ ————————

Mr. Todd was out with the neighbors. Even when she thought of him, Ms. Emily referred to her husband with a suffix before his name. Not being able to sleep, she headed down to the slave quarters to have one of them fix her something to help ease her mind. As she continued walking down the hall, she heard a noise, which grew louder as she approached. It was coming from the kitchen pantry. She opened the pantry door, and there was her husband with the slave girl Osana.

Osana reached out her hand, seeking help from Ms. Emily—hoping she could pull her husband away. Mr. Todd noticed his wife and commanded her to close the door of the pantry. Ms. Emily did as her husband requested and then walked back to their room. The rest of the night was spent with Ms. Emily filling her pillow with tears. *A different*

26

night, but the same evening, Ms. Emily thinks to herself. She thought her husband was done sleeping with the slave girls, but there was always one she seemed to have to scare away.

Ms. Emily treated the last slave girl that her husband cheated with such malice that she ran away. The family up the road found her washed up on the shore of the Savannah River. Everyone guessed that she became tired of running and decided to end her life. Now that Mr. Todd had found another, Ms. Emily began to plot how she would get rid of this one.

9 MONTHS LATER

꤮꤮꤮

Normally, Ms. Emily would take it easy on the pregnant slaves, but not Osana. Only in the presence of her husband did she subside her abuse. Osana remained respectful and obeyed every word of Ms. Emily. She knew she had to be strong not only for herself, but for her child as well, or else she'd end up like the other slave girl who Mr. Todd had raped. Osana's memories from back home helped her escape the abuse.

When it was time for Osana to give birth, her friend—a midwife on the plantation—helped her. Hearing the cry of a young child, Mr. Todd and Ms. Emily awoke and went to investigate. Upon looking at Osana's child, Ms. Emily became angry. The child was not of a darker skin tone, like most of the newborns, but had a lighter tone and shared many of her husband's features. Osana's husband looked on as well, hoping that it was his, but he knew from looking upon the child that it wasn't, but like most of the men on the plantation, they knew it wasn't their wives' fault.

Mr. Todd grinned and explained that he wanted the mess cleaned up by morning and returned to his room. Ms. Emily stood over the women, glaring at the mixed-race child. Her husband's child. She turned away slowly, uncertain of what she should do, or how she should feel—for all she felt was anger. For a moment, she thought about confronting her husband, but she remembered what happened last time; the marks from the slap took days to go away.

7 YEARS LATER

Ms. Emily watched Osana's daughter grow, and with every passing year, Ms. Emily's fury grew towards Osana and her daughter as well. She tormented Osana, referring to her child as a mulatto, provoking Osana to say otherwise, but she never did, although she wanted to. Though difficult for Osana's husband, he still treated the child as if she were his own. "*No child should feel that they don't have a father,*" he would explain, holding Osana and their daughter, Abioye.

When Osana was pregnant with Mr. Todd's child, it was bittersweet. She was happy to have been carrying life but ashamed of how that life came about. However, when she gave birth, her shame subsided. She did not care how her daughter came about, only that she was healthy. A beautiful baby with brown eyes—and lots and lots of hair.

One evening, Todd and Emily Filius had a gathering. The slaves were to prepare the meals and serve the guest. "Come on, Osana! We must start preparing! You're already on Ms. Emily's bad side—let us not make things worse!"

Osana looked over at her sister, Zilla. "I'm coming, but first, I must finish with Abby's hair," she said to her sister in their language. Osana's daughter had a head full of hair, and it often took Osana hours to complete.

Abioye looked up at her mother hoping that the tugging and braiding would soon be over. When she was younger, Abioye would run as soon as she got the chance, causing Osana to chase her across the field with a wooden brush in her hand, but as she got older, she gained the tolerance for it.

"All done!" Osana kissed Abioye on her forehead and jumped up. "Let's go, Zilla, before you lose control." Osana washed her hands, and they ran to the big house to assist the other slaves with preparing supper for this evening's extravaganza, and Abioye stayed behind playing with a doll her mother stitched for her.

PART II

It was halfway through dinner, and the party was going well—until a guest noticed a long strand of hair in her meal. She brought her findings to Ms. Emily, who apologized and said that she would have another plate brought to her expeditiously.

Later that evening, Mr. Todd left to be with his comrades up the road, leaving Ms. Emily alone with the slaves. She grabbed the cat o' nine tails from the shed and headed to the slave headquarters. They were now preparing their supper, and when they saw Ms. Emily with the whip, they all stopped and gave her their attention.

"Who does this belong to?" Ms. Emily asked, holding up the strand of hair.

The slaves do not make a sound.

"Cat's got your tongue—well, that's okay, I shall ask again." Ms. Emily paused and began walking around slowly, making her presence known to each slave she passed. "Whose is this?" she asked again.

Still, no sound was made by anyone.

Ms. Emily grabbed Zilla by her hair and dragged her to the middle of the room.

"Now, you niggers speak UP! Or I will whip her until she passes out before you!"

The slaves put their heads down.

"Okay, then!" Ms. Emily stripped Zilla down, raised the whip, and began to lash her. She cried out—a cry that filled the entire plantation.

"Stop, stop! It is mine. I was doing my daughter's hair, and it probably got on my clothes. I washed up, ma'am. I swear I didn't see it."

"Ah, Osana. Of course." Ms. Emily let Zilla free, and she ran to the corner to nurse her wounds.

"From now on, I don't want to see any slave with their hair out. You cover those heads, or I will cut your hair off! And you," she continued, pointing to Osana's daughter, "You come with me."

"No, Ms. Emily. Take me—please take me."

Ms. Emily grabbed Abioye and took off, dragging the little girl to her personal washroom, locking the door behind them.

She ordered the young girl to sit on the floor and place the back of her neck on the edge of the large porcelain basin, "put your head back," she told Abioye, while pouring water into it. She explained that she was going to wash her hair.

"Please don't, ma'am. My ma just did my hair, it will hurt if it's washed again," she pleaded.

"Don't worry, my dear child. It will not hurt for too long. Now, put your head back," Ms. Emily said, repeating herself.

Abioye did as Ms. Emily asked. A calmness came over Abioye as she sat there, listening to the pouring water. She knew Ms. Emily would not be able to take out her hair to wash it. So instead of panicking, she waited for her to give up. Ms. Emily continued filling the basin while Abioye's head rested against it. Her feet were crossed, along with her fingers, which were gently placed across her chest.

With help from the soothing sounds of water and exhaustion from crying, Abioye fell into a deep sleep, where she dreamed of red cardinals taking her to an extraordinary place. After a moment spent collecting herself and building her confidence, Ms. Emily took her husband's shaving blade and slit the young girl's throat.

When Mr. Todd came home that evening, he flew into a rage, seeing what his wife had done—and he beat her to the point of unconsciousness. While unconscious, Ms. Emily had a dream:

Ms. Emily arrived at a kingdom surrounded by a large gate, protected by guards of all shapes, sizes and color. She pulled, and pushed, but the gate refused to open.

"Let me in!" she demanded.

A small man came to the front of the gate, looking to see the lost soul that wanted to enter. "How may we help you, dear?" the gentlemen asked Ms. Emily.

"I don't know how you can help me. All I know is that I'm here, and I demand to be let in."

The gentlemen, Mr. Tuttle, took a good look at Emily. "May I have your name?"

"Mrs. Emily Filius," she said with pride.

Mr. Tuttle looked at his clipboard, lowering his glasses to see if her name was on his list. He flipped through the pages, looking back and forth between Ms. Emily and the pages. "You don't seem to be on my list. Let's find out why." He came out of the gate and led Ms. Emily to a tent not far from the gates that surrounded a kingdom.

The tent was larger than its outside appearance gave it credit for, and the inside was so dark that Ms. Emily could feel the darkness covering her skin. Mr. Tuttle lit a lamp and led her to a small corner that was covered with floor pillows and had incense burning, which gave the room a pleasant aroma.

"I need you to rest your head and put this over your face," said Mr. Tuttle, handing Ms. Emily a scarlet cloth. She did as Mr. Tuttle asked, and within seconds, she saw flashes of memories—even the memory of killing Osana's daughter, Abioye. It made Ms. Emily jump up, and she no longer wanted to be in the tent. "I demand to leave this place at once! Return me home this instant!" she demanded.

"You can leave, but then you will be lost. For there is no other home for you."

"What are you speaking of? Where do you live? I want to get into that kingdom behind those gates. Are you going to let me in, or what?"

"Madam, I apologize, but I cannot let you in. My orders are strict, and I must obey. If you are not on this list, I must bring you here to show you why you are not allowed in."

"Nonsense!" shouted Ms. Emily. She stormed out of the tent and headed back towards the large gate. Ms. Emily began pounding on it and screaming to be allowed in.

One of the guards protecting the gate approached Ms. Emily. "I must ask that you stop shouting. This is a place of peace, ma'am," the guard explained to Emily.

"To hell with your peace! I want in! Let me in!" Ms. Emily shouted.

Mr. Tuttle was behind Ms. Emily, watching her make a spectacle of herself.

He raised his hand, and with one snap, Ms. Emily's mouth disappeared, causing her to be silent.

"Now, let me explain this to you, Madam Emily. I do not know why you are not allowed in. It is not my place to know your assignment and how you have failed, but what I do know is that you are not getting in no matter what mockery you make of yourself. Now, you have two options: For the first, you can head back to the tent with me and obtain your new assignment to be allowed back in. Or you walk around the Land of Aimlessness. No purpose, no path—just out here, alone." He said pointing to the empty void that laid ahead.

Mr. Tuttle snapped his fingers after he understood that Ms. Emily comprehended the full scope of what he was explaining.

Ms. Emily, with a much calmer tone, stated, "I don't know of an assignment. All I know is that I'm tired and need to rest. There must be a mistake. Is there someone I can speak to?"

"If that were an option, I would have told you so. What do you choose? Tent for a new assignment or aimless living?" asked Mr. Tuttle.

Ms. Emily chose to handle things her own way and decided on aimless living, walking away from the kingdom. The further she walked, the colder it became. After what felt like hours, she came across a group of people who were all standing around a fire to keep warm. She was hesitant about walking over, but she did anyway, happy to see faces.

"Hello, my name is Emily. Do you guys stay around here?" Emily asked in hopes of making conversation.

"I do," said one of the men around the fire. "My family and I stay not too far from here. Do you need somewhere to rest your head?"

"If you don't mind, that would be great. I need to find a way back home. I was trying to enter a place surrounded by these large gates. It reminded me of a castle, but they wouldn't let me in, and now I need to find a way back home."

"Oh, lost, huh—I was lost for a while, but then I just stopped trying and decided to make this my home," said another man.

"And what exactly is this place?" she asked.

"We are still trying to figure that out."

The man who offered to let Ms. Emily stay with him and his family introduced himself as Sono.

PART III

Sono's home was a large cave, covered in different artwork and symbols.

"Here we are" said Sono, opening the entry way for them to enter. When Ms. Emily entered the home, she was greeted by Sono's wife and daughter.

"Torethsha, honey, we have a guest," said Sono. Torethsha was a tall woman, with long dark hair and eyes that intimidated anyone she stared at. She did not walk, she glided, and was not shy about wearing little no matter who was around.

"And you are?"

"This is Ms. Emily." Said Sono

"Is she not able to speak?" said Torethsha staring at Ms. Emily.

"My name is Mrs. Emily Filius, and your husband was kind enough to let me stay with you all because I didn't have anywhere to go."

Torethsha nods, "Well of course, my husband must see something in you to allow you here." She then focuses her attention on her husband Sono, "Zejebel and I are heading to Earth. We're bored." Zejebel, their daughter stands next to her mother with dark makeup covering her face, and though she was younger, she too took after her mother in terms of clothing. Zejebel said nothing to Ms. Emily or her father as she left with her mother.

"Teens huh… what are you going to do?" said Sono laughing, easing the tension he knew she felt after being in the presence of his wife and child.

Once Torethsha and Zejebel left, Sono did not waste any time.

"So, tell me, Ms. Emily, what has you lingering amongst these parts?"

"I don't know. I was trying to get through this gate, and for the life of me, I don't understand why I wanted to so badly when what I need is to go home."

"Did you get a chance to meet Tuttle?" asked Sono. "He's the one at the gate."

"Yes, we've met, what is this place?"

"Did he bring you into the Tent of Truth?" asked Sono, ignoring Ms. Emily's question.

Ms. Emily looked at him. "Is that what that place is called, yes he did; how did you know?"

"Everyone walking around the Land of Aimlessness has been there. We got the same ultimatum that you were given, tent for a new assignment for another opportunity to get through the gate or walk and become lost in this land. Except not all of us are lost."

"I just want to go home."

"I can make that happen."

"How?!" Ms. Emily asked without noticing Sono's sinister smile.

"First, tell me what was revealed to you in that tent," he asked, intently awaiting her response.

"Why does that matter?"

"Well, to help you, I must understand why you weren't let in the gate in the first place. That reason was revealed to you in the tent, and I must know it."

"I killed the daughter of one of my slaves."

Sono looked at Emily, now smiling from ear to ear.

"Well, well… a murderer in my very own home. It's no wonder you couldn't get through the gate."

Sono walked around his cave, pondering. "Why did you kill her?"

Ms. Emily lowers her head. "My husband fathered her, and I hated the little girl for it."

"So, you just decided to kill her?"

"It was a multitude of things," said Ms. Emily, becoming agitated with the constant questioning.

Sono noticed Ms. Emily's discomfort and decided to continue his probe anyway. "I don't get it. You just walked past her and decided that today was the day? I'm going to need more details if you want my help."

"She and her mother tried embarrassing me at one of my events. Instead of taking the time to make sure she was proper, she rushed in with her daughter's hair all over her clothes. I needed to make an example; plus, I was tired of having to watch her grow up in my face. All the neighbors knew. I could see it in their faces. I was embarrassed and tired of being disrespected in my own home."

"I understand being embarrassed and needing to make an example, but why did her having her daughter's hair on her clothes upset you?" asked Sono.

"Because a strand of hair got into one of my guest's meals."

"I see, so, how did you kill her?" asked Sono, intrigued.

"I slit her throat,"

Ms. Emily said nothing as she waited for Sono's response.

"Stone cold, aren't yah? I like it. But I will tell you this, the Ruler isn't allowing you in his kingdom after the act you did, but don't fear, Sono's here. Now, what you did was unforgivable, but there is a way I can get you to make amends with the Ruler of the kingdom to get you in."

"I don't care about getting into the kingdom; I care about going home."

"Well, you just made my task a bit easier. I will send you back to your home, but you will need to bring me a child. You help me, and I will help you. The child has to give you the exact same feeling of the child you murdered."

"Well, that should be easy. We have plenty on our plantation."

Sono let out a laugh. "That would be too easy."

He snapped his fingers.

Ms. Emily awoke in a small Harlem apartment on E. 125th in the late 1950s. She tried to get up, but the pain from her lower back quickly laid her back down. She looked around the room, not recognizing it. Next to her was a nightstand, holding up a lamp with a ripped shade.

She turned on the lamp to get a better view of her surroundings and notices a newspaper on the nightstand, with a headline that read, "Negro Boy Killed For 'Wolf Whistle.'" Ms. Emily quickly knew that she was not in her home and that time had changed.

When she managed to get herself up, she found the bathroom in the tiny apartment to look at her appearance. An older version of her former self looked back, and her appearance brought Ms. Emily to tears.

"What is this?! Where am I?!" she shouted, confused, before heading for the door. Before she was able to open it, out of nowhere, Sono appeared.

"Where are you off to?" he asked, noticing her breakdown.

"What have you done to me?! You said you would bring me home! This is not my home!"

"Well, your definition of home was vague. Technically you are home. You're not in the Land of Aimlessness anymore, are you?"

"But I wanted to be home, with my husband, on my land."

"Yes, yes, with your many slaves that you enjoy torturing. But, unfortunately, time was not on your side, and I'm sure your husband didn't miss you."

Emily continued to sob as she spoke, "You don't know my husband, and you don't know me. This is not my life. I looked out the window, and slaves everywhere!

Walking around like you and me. And what is this?" She says grabbing the newspaper that was on the nightstand. What is a negro?" All these tall places. Where am I?" cried Emily.

Sono explained to her how time had changed, and how she would need to conduct herself to fit in—until she found the child for Sono, of course.

"How will I be able to walk out there and find what it is that's needed to bring me home?" asked Emily.

"I keep telling you that you are home, but if you want to go back into your old life, that's all you had to say."

"Yes, Sono," said Emily, annoyed. "I will find the child, and then you will return me to my old life; my old home" She locked eyes with Sono to make sure they agreed.

"Done," proclaimed Sono. "There's an old art studio that was turned into a school. I would start there if I were you."

AFRO NIA

Meets

MS. FILIUS

AFRO NIA MEETS MS. FILIUS

$\smile\ 2\ 6\ 6\ \smile$

M s. Emily, who had not seen anything like Harlem, struggled, but was determined to get back to her old life. She did as Sono said and started working at the school as a cafeteria lady. The children at the school reminded her of the children on the plantation. To avoid showing her true colors, she kept quiet and did her job. She saw children who resembled the one she murdered in her former life, but none of them gave her the same feeling she had when she first laid eyes on Abioye—until a transfer student arrived.

After weeks of watching the young girl, Ms. Emily finally decided to ask her what her name was.

"Nia," said the first grader. "But everyone calls me Afro Nia because my hair is so big," she said, giggling. "What is your name?"

"You call me Ms. Filius," Emily said to the young girl. She knew that she found the child who would redeem her and bring her back to her normal life. All she needed to do was get Afro Nia alone, and the deed would be done. Ms. Emily patiently waited until the opportunity presented itself.

AFRO NIA

Nia was born to a farmer and seamstress who decided to move to the big city to open their own cleaning business. While she enjoyed helping her parents on the farmland, she heard amazing stories about the city and could not wait to experience it. Aside from assisting her parents, Afro Nia also loved playing with her pup, Deeno.

While Afro Nia was playing outside her parents' shop, an old woman came over and began to stare. Deeno ran towards the woman, barking, and Afro Nia's mother, Candace, came outside when she heard their dog.

"Hello," Afro Nia said, recognizing the old woman as the cafeteria lady. Emily continued to stare at Afro Nia—as well as her hair—and then said, "Hello Afro Nia, playing outside today?"

"May I help you?" Afro Nia's mother interjected.

"How rude of me. I am Ms. Filius; I work at Afro Nia's school. I've always complimented your daughter on how beautiful her hair is."

"Go wait inside with Deeno," Afro Nia's mom said to her daughter, feeling uneasy about this woman staring at her daughter. Afro Nia did as her mother requested and waved bye to Ms. Filius.

"Nice to meet you, Ms. Filius, and thank you—she does get a lot of compliments on her ha—"

Ms. Filius walked away while Afro Nia's mother was mid-sentence.

"That's weird," mumbled Candace, still looking in Ms. Filius' direction while heading back inside her shop.

"What's wrong, hun?" Afro Nia's dad, Isaiah, asked, noticing her puzzled expression.

"Nothing—just had a strange encounter when one of the staff members from Nia's school. She was just staring at our daughter and then walks away while I was speaking to her."

"Don't worry yourself over it; did Nia seem bothered?"

"No, she wasn't. She was happy to see her."

"See? Don't over-analyze," Isaiah said, trying to comfort his wife. Isaiah and Candance continued with their work while Afro Nia and Pup Deeno played in the backyard of the shop.

WEEKS LATER

It was Friday, and the three o'clock bell was only ten minutes away from ringing. Afro Nia's teacher brought the class into the schoolyard and waited for each parent to arrive. It was down to two students—Afro Nia and another student, and then eventually, it was just Afro Nia.

Emily walked over, seeing Afro Nia and her teacher, and said, "Hey, Ms. Nelly, if you want, I can take her to the office to call her parents."

Ms. Nelly looked at Afro Nia and asked if it was okay if Ms. Filius escorted her to the office to call her parents. Afro Nia nodded her head, agreeing.

"Okay, give me a hug," Ms. Nelly said.

Afro Nia hugged her teacher and walked with Ms. Filius. As they headed for the office, Ms. Emily began talking, trying to ease her own tension, "So, tell me, how's first grade going?"

"It's going good. I just do not understand why we must always learn something new. The moment I learn one thing, I forget the other," Afro Nia explained.

Half listening, Emily suddenly said, "Oh dear, I forgot something in the cafeteria. Would you mind coming with me before we head to the office?"

Afro Nia agreed.

"I believe I left it just down there." Ms. Filius opened a door leading to the cafeteria cellar and started heading down the stairs. "Come down with me, I don't want to leave you up there by yourself." Afro Nia reluctantly looked down the stairs, decided to trust Ms. Filius, and followed.

Once Afro Nia passed Ms. Filius, she pushed her down the stairs and shut the door. Nia had just picked herself up off the floor as Ms. Filius reached the bottom of the stairs.

"I want my mommy and daddy, Ms. Filius. What are you doing? Why am I down here?"

"Don't worry about it, my dear. It'll all be over soon."

Afro Nia looked at Ms. Filius, her face covered in horror. "What will all be over soon?"

"Don't worry about that. Now, be a good girl, and sit down."

Emily called on Sono.

Afro Nia looked around to see who Ms. Filius was calling. Within minutes, Sono appeared.

"Look, Sono! I have done what you asked me!" she said, pointing at Afro Nia in the corner.

Sono slowly walked over to Afro Nia. "Well now—hello little girl," he said, observing Afro Nia as she lay with her head in her lap, scared and crying.

"Okay, there she is. Now return me."

"I'm afraid we have a problem," said Sono.

"No, Sono. What we have is an agreement."

"I'm unable to take this child. She's protected," said Sono, still observing the young girl, fascinated at the guard around her—a guard only individuals like Sono can see.

"Protected? Look, I've done what you asked, now return me," said Emily.

"Well, Ms. Emily, if this young girl brings about the same feelings that you felt back when you committed your crime, then yes, you have done it, but you took that other girl's life, so I would need a life to trade, and I'm unable to take this one, but you may if you still have it in you."

Angered, Emily grabbed a pair of scissors from a shelf. She pulled Afro Nia from the corner and began cutting out the puffs from her hair while shouting, "It was the hair that caused me to kill, so here! Use this and return me now!"

Emily handed the hair to Sono.

"Run along, little girl, and stop crying, it'll grow back," Sono said to Afro Nia. Afro Nia ran out of the basement in search of help, still crying and now covering her head with her scarf so no one could see that her hair had been cut.

Sono returned his attention to Emily while still holding Afro Nia's hair.

"Trust me, your reason for killing was deeper than hair, but for you, Ms. Emily, I'll make an exception. I'm sure you're ready to return to your life, correct?"

"Yes! Now! Please!" demanded Emily. Sono smiled and snapped his fingers.

AFRO NIA – PART II

"NIA!" a voice called from a distance. Afro Nia turned around and saw her mother and father rushing towards her. She ran to them, still crying.

"What happened, where were you? Are you hurt?" Afro Nia pulled her scarf from off her head to show them her hair. "Who did this?!" demanded her parents.

"It was Ms. Filius," cried Afro Nia.

"The woman from the shop earlier, where is she?" demanded her parents. Afro Nia pointed to the basement. Without hesitation, Afro Nia's dad ran to the basement and tried opening the door, but it was jammed shut.

Afro Nia's mother called the police and headed to the office to see if there were any school staff still inside, but there was no one. When the police arrived, they managed to get the basement door open, but there was no one down there. No Emily Filius and no Sono.

Within weeks, Afro Nia's hair begun to grow back. Her mother and father were happy to have their daughter, seeing how close they came to almost losing her. Afro Nia explained what happened to her parents and to the police, but Ms. Filius was nowhere to be found, and the case grew cold.

Afro Nia, though traumatized, was able to continue with life with her parents and Pup Deeno, and the events of that evening soon became a distant memory, but they still had a way of haunting her every so often.

BACK TO MS. EMILY

Ms. Emily awoke in her bed, relieved that the nightmare was over. She tried walking, but could not; she tried talking, but couldn't. A slave came into the room and saw that Ms. Emily had opened her eyes.

"Sir!" the young girl shouted. "It's Ms. Emily! She opened her eyes!"

Mr. Todd walked into the room to see his wife, and the young girl left, allowing them to be alone and he sat beside her. "Well, nice to have you back. You are probably confused, so I'll explain. You killed Osana's daughter, whom I was fond of, leaving Osana to run off with her nigger husband. When I saw what you did, I beat you senseless—to the point where you have severe damage to the brain. Particularly the parts of the brain that deal with locomotion and speech.

"Luckily, the sheriff didn't do much of an investigation when I told them that you had fallen down the stairs. I guess I owe that to you; you always did like to have them over at our big parties. His wife also made a pie for when you feel better. She also wanted me to tell you not to get so worked up about the hair incident. It didn't disturb her fun that night, not one bit."

Mr. Todd looked into his wife's eyes to see if she understood what he was saying. He could see she did. "But like I said, nice to have you back home. I'll be sure that the slaves tend to you." Mr. Todd then walked out of the room, calling his slave back in to tend to Ms. Emily.

Ms. Emily was a vegetable. Unable to eat, walk, or talk after waking up from her coma. One evening as she lay, she tried calling out to Sono for help. To her surprise, he heard her and came at once, almost as if he were waiting. "You wanted your life back, and you got it." Just like that, Sono disappeared into the darkness, leaving Ms. Emily to reflect on her actions and her part in contributing to the evil in the world.

She lived the rest of her life with the slaves; they pushed her from room to room, cleaned her, and tube fed her. She had no children and watched her husband make plenty with the women of the plantation.

QUEEN NILAH

QUEEN NILAH

⁓ ◑ ◐ ⌐

There is a faraway land where the royals live—a land where you are given the title king and queen but must prove yourself worthy through your assignments to keep it. Among the royals was a being by the name of Queen Nilah, who, unlike the other queens, was not as confident, and often second-guessed herself. She prided herself on her commitment to helping others whenever she could, and she spent her time cultivating her garden. It was mid-day when the sound of trumpets from the Ruler's Palace filled the land. The sound of the horn meant that the Ruler was going to be giving a speech, and all those living within the palace grounds were to attend. Within minutes, people from all over had begun to gather.

"Has anyone gotten any word of what will be discussed?" asked Queen Nilah to one of the bystanders.

"It's rumored that the Ruler will pick a wife for his son, King Melchez," the woman said, trying to make her way to the front of the crowd to get a better view of the Ruler. Queen Nilah followed along with her.

Moments later, the Ruler and his many sons came out onto the palace balcony. The crowd calmed themselves at the sight of his presence. The Ruler took a minute to admire the beautiful souls before him and then spoke: "Welcome! As you all know, my son, Melchez, is now ready to lead and accept a queen. Though they are many wonderful queens throughout the kingdom, I can pick just one, and—along with his help, of course—we have found the one who is right for him."

Agents came down from the palace to crown the chosen to rule alongside King Melchez. As the agents got closer to Queen Nilah, she continued to think that they were going to approach one of the women standing aside her, but not her. The agent held the crown over Queen Nilah, and the crowd cheered and raised her up in celebration. Though excited, Queen Nilah was taken aback, and her excitement turned into fear, thinking of the responsibility that came with such an honor; she was uncertain if she was ready to join the Royal family.

All chosen wives were allowed to take time to decide whether they wanted to accept the union, but most immediately saw the privilege of marrying one of the sons of the Ruler; but Queen Nilah requested that she have some time to think over the proposal. She knew that she did not want to disappoint her Ruler but wanted to make sure she was truly ready. As time passed without an answer from Queen Nilah, the Ruler sent his daughter to check on her.

"How's it going?" asked Princess Noni.

Queen Nilah knew the true reason for Princess Noni's visit and did not hesitate to address the elephant.

"Did the Ruler send you?

"Whoa, I always check up on you, Nilah. This has nothing to do with my father or my brother, Melchez."

"Oh no?" said Queen Nilah smiling at Princess Noni.

"Well, maybe it does. Why are you taking so long to decide? My brother is smitten. He wants you for his wife. Got him pacing back and forth, sweating," said Noni laughing.

"I know, and I'm flattered, but it's a big step, and comes with major responsibilities."

"Well, I know you are ready, and plus, I know you'll are great for one another," said Princess Noni, hugging Queen Nilah.

After Princess Noni's visit, Queen Nilah knew she had a serious decision to make and did not want to waste any more time. She arrived at the palace and first showed honor and thanks to the Ruler for choosing her. She was then escorted by one of the royal agents to her private room, where maidens awaited her to get ready for the marriage to King Melchez. Though she was nervous, she only showed grace, confidence, and honor while preparing for her union with the king, and everyone in the kingdom was in attendance.

After only spending a little time together, Queen Nilah was not disappointed with her decision and fell madly in love with the king the Ruler set for her.

AN ETERNITY LATER

‐ꙅꙅ‐

As Queen Nilah and King Melchez slept, they were awakened by a loud knock at their door. The king got out of bed to answer and then returned, holding a notice from the Royal Palace. The king and queen became worried, for they know a messenger delivering a notice from the palace this late could only mean that one of them had been called for an assignment.

"King, what is that you have in your hand? Have you been summoned?" asked Nilah.

"No, my queen, this notice is for you…"

The queen felt her heart sink to the ground and beat rapidly as she read:

> *Queen Nilah:*
>
> *A being full of wisdom, strength, and structure.*
>
> *You have been called to complete an assignment. Report to the meeting ground at the sound of the first horn.*
>
> *–The Ruler*

The two hugged and spent their last night together—in love, in peace, and in harmony.

At the sound of the horn, the king and queen headed to the meeting ground to say their goodbyes. There awaited the souls of the kingdom, ready to say their goodbyes to Queen Nilah. She noticed Princess Noni;

her cheeks were covered in tears that had been wiped away. Seeing this, Queen Nilah ran to Noni, and they hugged and cried together.

"You are my sister," said the queen, "and if the Ruler sees fit, he will have you join me. If not, I'll be back soon. No need to be saddened, princess. I will carry you in my heart."

The two let go of each other, and the queen continued saying her goodbyes to the rest of the souls.

"Beware of the evil that is down there," said one of her comrades.

"Be aware that the enemy will be after you," said another.

"Stay positive and remember the word of our Ruler," said a third.

Then she said her last goodbyes to her kingly husband. "I'm deeply saddened that you will not be joining me on this journey. Not knowing or remembering you seems unbelievable. Not feeling your touch or having you near—my heart will cry out for you," said the queen.

"Our Ruler will be watching over you, and when he sees fit, I will come to be with you. Don't be saddened, my queen. You are strong, and our Ruler needs you. Make him proud. I will miss you every moment, and hopefully, he'll send me to you when the time is right." They gave each other one last hug, and the queen waved goodbye to the other royals before entering the kingdom, where her Ruler awaited her.

Queen Nilah walked down the path that led to the Ruler's throne. He stood as she approached, and she bowed her head.

"Queen Nilah!"

"Yes, Ruler," she said, head still bowed.

"Are you ready for your assignment," the Ruler said as he descended from his throne.

"Yes, Ruler. I am ready."

"Ready for what, Queen Nilah?" said the Ruler as he took a step towards her.

"Ready to help spread light and love."

"Will you be tricked by the enemy?" said the Ruler as he took another step.

"No, my Ruler," responded Queen Nilah.

"Why not, queen?" Another step.

"Because I know your word is true, Ruler. I know the enemy is only there to trap me and to laugh at me later. I know the enemy will use me to upset you. He wants nothing more to separate me from you." She took a deep breath. "You are the Ruler of all Rulers, and it is you whom I follow."

The Ruler, now closer, told Queen Nilah to raise her head and to look him in his eye. "I will continue to watch over you." He took her hand and led her to the Lake of Purity located behind the Ruler's palace. "Remember these words and remember these feelings; whenever in doubt, look inside yourself, and you will find me. I will get you through."

"Yes, Ruler." The queen bowed and then dove into the Lake of Purity, where she was stripped of her identity, leaving her with just her soul.

PART II

⸺⸺⸺⸺⸺⸺⸺⸺⸺⸺

BROOKLYN - 1993

Anajah was a fourteen-year-old teen who lived with her grandmother Ruth, in Brooklyn, New York. Their household was strict but still filled with much love. Though Ruth took good care of her, Anajah still longed for a mother and father. Not having them around made her feel misplaced. Her grandmother had told her little about her parents when Anajah asked questions about them; Ruth's only comments were that they loved music and were often touring, which was why they were not around. *Not a phone call, anything to see how I'm doing,* Anajah would often write in her journal, the only place she felt safe to express her true self.

It was a beautiful Saturday morning; the rays from the sun peeked through Anajah's window, waking her up. "*Thank you for waking me up,*" she said, speaking to the Ruler while reaching her hands up to the ceiling. She noticed the time and wondered why her nanna hadn't woken her up to clean yet. Normally, by this hour, Ruth would be wide awake, playing her spirituals, singing along, with a broom in her hand. Anajah pulled herself out of bed to check on her grandmother and could hear coughing as she got closer to her bedroom.

She knocks on her grandmother's door, "Why aren't we up yet?" she said, peaking her head into her grandmother's bedroom. Ruth was still tucked in, with the room filling with smoke from the vaporizer smelling like Bengay and Vick's Rub.

"Not feeling well, nanna?"

"No, baby, not at all," said her grandmother.

"Don't worry. I'm here. I can clean up and make breakfast."

"You're a sweet girl Anajah. Your grandfather would be as proud of you as I am."

Paul was Anajah's grandfather, a stubborn man who died doing what he loved, fishing. He was told by the men on the dock that the tides were too strong for him to be out on the water, but Paul did not heed their warning, determined to catch his fish. The news of his passing hit Ruth and Anajah hard, and after seven years, Ruth still included his name in her daily speech.

Ruth managed to get herself out of bed and went into her closet, bringing out a box with daisy designs. She opened it and pulled out a letter, still neatly folded. "I saved this for you. Your mother left it in the crib for you the night she left," said Ruth, handing Anajah the letter.

Anajah waited a second before taking it. She thought about opening it, but felt she wasn't ready. Ruth noticed the sorrow that overtook Anajah, holding a letter from a mother who had abandoned her. The night Anajah's mother left, she knew her granddaughter would be left with a void only her parents would be able to fill, and it hurt her to see her granddaughter be saddened by the actions of her parents.

"The hardest part about life is forgiving people who have wronged you, but you forgive them for yourself, not for them," Ruth explained.

Anajah tucked her grandmother back in bed and spent the weekend catering to her grandmother and debating with herself if she should read her mother's goodbye letter.

TWO WEEKS LATER

────────────── ⟋⟍⟋⟍ ──────────────

It was lunchtime, and Anajah and her best friend Naomi were sitting in their school's cafeteria. They often sat by themselves, not feeling like they were a part of the rest of the school, and they preferred it that way. Their friendship began when Naomi defended Anajah from a bully named Trish, who started picking on Anajah because of the clothes she wore.

"Pretty yes, but those clothes, dear." Trish, along with the two girls with her, began to laugh. Anajah rolled her eyes and walked away, tying not to let Trish's words affect her.

Naomi overheard the rude comment while she was standing by her locker. "Hey, scarecrow, did you ever get that brain?" she shouted at Trish.

"I know you're not talking to me," Trish said, turning around.

"Yeah, I am. You need those clothes to conceal that empty skull."

Trish raised her middle finger and walked off with her friends.

"You didn't have to defend me. I ignore them."

"It's all good. I was looking for a reason to tell them off. Walking around here like they own the place," Naomi said, laughing.

That was sixth grade, and now in ninth, the girls were as close as ever.

"I couldn't wait to show you. I finally finished it," said Naomi pulling out a twelve-by-twelve latch hook of a tabby cat.

"Oh, wow! Look how beautiful it came out!"

"Thank you, thank you," said Naomi as if she just won a pageant.

"You should hang it up right over your bed."

"I thought about that, but I have enough hanging up in my room, so this is for you."

"For me?!" Anajah jumped up and hugged Naomi, "Thank you so much."

On her way home from school, all Anajah could think about was where she was going to hang up the latch hook her best friend had given to her. As she approached her home, she noticed the ambulance parked in front of it.

"*Nanna!*" she screamed upon seeing her grandmother being put unto a stretcher with an oxygen mask covering her face.

The detective saw Anajah standing in the middle of the street, her hands covering her mouth and breaking down in tears.

"Are you Anajah?" he asked, approaching her.

"I am."

"Why don't you come inside and have a seat. Your grandmother mentioned you would be coming home soon."

"What happened to my grandmother?"

"Please, Anajah, come inside and take a seat."

Anajah did as the detective said and sat in the living room, where a woman awaited her. Anajah continued looking at the detective, still waiting for a response. The woman stood up and introduced herself. "Hello Anajah, my name is Ms. King, and I'm a child advocate. I know this is a lot for you to handle, but we will work together to get you through this. Is there any family that we can call?"

"Can someone please tell me what happened!" Anajah said, becoming frustrated.

"Your grandmother is not in the best condition. We need to call a family member right away."

Anajah got up, ran to her room, and locked the door. She dropped to her knees and pleaded: *"Please, Ruler, please don't take my nanna from me, too. Please, please don't take my nanna from me. I will do anything you ask of me. I've been good. I help around as much as I can. Ruler, please take pity on me. Please do not turn your back. Please, Ruler. Heal her."*

With tears still filling her eyes, Anajah got up to get the letter written by her mother. She could still hear Ms. King and the detective knocking at the door, but her grief tuned them out. Anajah went under her comforter, folded into the fetal position, and read her letter:

My Daughter Anajah,

Deciding to leave you has been the hardest decision I ever had to make.

When you were born to me,

I stopped doubting if the Ruler thought profoundly of me or not.

I just wish I were able to see what he does.

And I am searching to find out what that is, and I cannot find it if I stay.

Do not hate me for having to leave. Your grandparents will give you what you need until it is time for us to meet again.

Love Always,

Your mother, Denise

PART III

Ms. King worked hard on tracking down the biological parents of Anajah, using hospital records she was able to obtain. Due to Ruth having to remain in the hospital, Anajah was placed in a temporary home for girls until they could locate a relative who was willing to take her in. On the way to her temporary placement, Anajah tried imagining that she was in a pond, floating like the lily pads that surrounded her to escape her reality. It was this very thought that was interrupted when the bus came to a halt.

There stood a tall, six-story brick building, which seemed to be an old hospital turned into a covenant for young girls without a home. The place looked dark to Anajah; the windows were huge, and Anajah could see girls looking out their window from their rooms, observing the new girls getting off the bus. To Anajah, the place looked more like a prison than a haven.

"This is us," said Ms. King, who was sitting beside Anajah. She got up, grabbed Anajah's belongings from above them, and they got off the bus. Anajah could feel all the girls staring at her, sizing her up and down. When they entered, guards greeted them and told them to put their coats and belongings on the conveyer belt to go through scanning. Anajah looked around and was even more terrified, hoping that this was not the place she was staying.

"Am I staying here?" Anajah asked Ms. King as they went through the metal detectors.

"It's only temporary," said Ms. King, not wanting to look directly at Anajah, feeling bad that she had to leave her in such a place.

Anajah was assigned to a small room on the fifth floor. There were three bathrooms on each floor, which were shared by the girls. She was given bed sheets, along with a box full of toiletries and snacks, and a list of rules. As she was making up her bed, she heard a knock at her door. Anajah opened it to see a group of girls standing in her doorway.

"Looks like you're getting comfortable," said one of the girls as they entered Anajah's room. The first one to speak introduced herself as Nicki.

"Yeah, it's pretty late, so I just want to go to sleep," said Anajah.

"You must be used to sleeping in such places, the way you're getting comfortable so easily."

"No, just tired and trying not to think about it."

"You gotta be dumb to not think about it."

Anajah did not respond to Nicki's rude comment and explained that she would like to get her rest, hinting for the girls to go. They did, along with something they had stolen without Anajah realizing.

She lay on her freshly made bed and thought of how she could brighten up her room, so she hung the latch hook over her bed and put her mother's letter underneath her pillow after reading it again. Her room was small, and it was in the corner of the building. It had two huge windows, a dresser, a full-size bed, and a small refrigerator. Though her windows were big, all she could see was a grey sky, as well as the windows that stared back at hers. Her memories brought her to her grandmother in a hospital somewhere, alone. The memories overwhelmed Anajah and brought her to tears, crying herself to sleep.

The next morning, Anajah woke up and had to blink twice to realize that she was not home. She picked herself up and got ready to head to the showers. In front of the bathroom, she noticed girls snickering, but didn't think anything of it. Anajah opened the bathroom door, almost hitting the girls who were on the other side of it, as they were fixated on whatever was on the other side. Not wanting to associate herself with what had everyone chattering, Anajah continued with her shower. When she was the only one left in the bathroom, she decided to peek at what the other girls had been focused on. *"It can't be,"* she thought, ripping the taped paper from the wall.

She ran into her room in search of her journal, but it was nowhere to be found, proving her worst fears true. She ran down the hallway, still in her towel, and discovered her journal's ripped pages taped all over the facility for all to see. Anajah pulled as much as she could from off the walls and spent the rest of her day in her room, crying. She knew it was Nicki and the two girls, for they were the only ones in her room.

Two weeks in the home for girls was enough for Anajah. She had not heard anything from Ms. King, or the detective regarding her mother, and Nicki and her friends wouldn't stop harassing her, causing her to isolate herself in her room. It was a Thursday when Ms. King came to do her weekly follow-up. Anajah came down to the meeting room, still in a big tea shirt and sweatpants, with her hair tied up, and dark circles underneath her eyes. Anajah sat across from Ms. King, with her head still lowered.

"How are you today, Anajah?"

"I don't want to be here anymore," said Anajah, getting straight to how she was feeling.

"Talk to me; tell me what's going on."

Noticing that Nicki's friends were nearby, she remained silent, not wanting to get caught telling, then deal with them later.

"It's nothing. I just don't feel like myself—that's all."

"Hang in there, Anajah. I'm working hard to get you out of this place."

The facility provided food for the girls, and after weeks of isolating herself because of embarrassment, Anajah decided to stay in the cafeteria to eat instead of bringing her food back to her room. She sat in the corner and picked at her plate, wishing she were back at school, having lunch with her best friend, Naomi. It didn't take long for Nicki to come over, with the same two girls who had entered her room. They sat down across from Anajah.

"Where have you been hiding?" asked Nicki with a smug tone.

Anajah, still picking at her plate, did not respond.

"Oh, I know what's gotten you down." Nicki pulled out Anajah's journal and starts dangling it in front of her. "Looking for this?"

Looking at her journal, ripped up and handled as if it was an old rag, infuriated Anajah. A feeling took over, a feeling that was unlike her natural calm and meek demeanor.

Then, Nicki began reading from the journal. "Dear Diary, though I know my grandmother loves me, I sometimes feel that her love isn't enough…"

"Nicki, give me back my journal!" Anajah shouted.

Nicki stopped reading, taken back by Anajah's tone. "Gosh, I'm just playing, take your stupid diary," she said, throwing it at Anajah and laughing.

Anajah could not hold back; she wanted to rip Nicki apart. The anger she kept buried inside began spilling over, for all to see, like her diary. Still sitting across from one another, Anajah jumped up on the table and lunged at her. Overtaken by anger, Anajah attacked Nicki, punching, kicking, and biting until security pulled her off Nicki, who was now curled up in the fetal position, protecting herself.

The home called Ms. King, who rushed to the facility right away, and Anajah was held in the counseling center until she arrived. Though Anajah stood up for herself, she couldn't help but cry. She thought she would feel good to have won her first fight, but there was something deep within her that was hurt about having to resort to violence.

When Ms. King arrived, she saw Anajah, crying, and ran to her aid right away. "Where are you hurt? Let me see your face—have the medics checked you out yet?"

"Yes, I'm fine."

"They called me and said you had a fight. Where are you hurt?"

"I'm not hurt, and they said I was fine."

"Okay, so why are you crying?

Anajah shrugged. "I don't know."

Ms. King smiled, admiring Anajah's heart. "Listen, it's okay to defend yourself. You just have to learn to do so with your words and not your fist." Ms. King handed Anajah tissue to wipe her face.

"I don't know how to use my words, Ms. King, and these girls only respond to violence."

"Life will teach you. The Ruler will send people, the right people to show you."

Anajah took a second to allow Ms. King's advice to sink in. "How's my grandmother, and did you hear from my mother yet?"

"Your grandmother is fine. She's just not well enough to return home, and yes, I was able to get in contact with your mother."

Anajah's eyes lit up. "Yes! Is she coming to get me?"

"We're working on that. Just give it a few more days."

FOURTH WEEK OF BEING IN THE HOME FOR GIRLS

———————⟋ و و ⟍———————

It was Thursday, and Anajah was in the rec room with the rest of the girls playing knock hockey. Since the fight, the girls had started warming up to Anajah, all except Nicki and her clique. She liked that they wanted to be friends with her, but she kept them at a distance. It was as if no one even cared or remembered the journal incident.

"Come! There's a crazy woman yelling at security!" said one of the girls as she came running from the hallway.

Anajah and the rest of the girls ran to see the commotion.

"Listen, I'm not trying to hear that. Bring me my child!" said the furious woman. She wore a sheer hot pink long gown that partly showed her cleavage and much of her back.

"Whoa, straight off the runway. Look at that outfit," said one of the girls in admiration.

"Ma'am, we already told you. We can't just let you see your child without the proper pass, and if not, you must have your child's advocate with you." A member of the security team touched the woman's shoulder to have her exit.

"Don't you put those filthy hands on me!"

"Ma'am, if you don't leave, I will have to call the police."

"Call them! My lawyer is in the car. I will be out of custody by the morning, and I'll be back, and with cameras! Look at this place. It's filthy! And you house young girls here! A pity!"

Another security guard frantically came out of his office.

"Look, ma'am, we contacted your daughter's advocate. As soon as she arrives, we can let you meet with your daughter."

"Fine. I'll stand right here until she comes." The woman noticed the girls looking on, and upon seeing Anajah, she took a second to notice her features. "Anajah! My precious baby." The girls gasped in disbelief that the woman was Anajah's mother. Anajah stood frozen, not knowing what to feel, having this be the first time she laid eyes on her mother. As Anajah stared, a variety of emotions filled her. She was happy at first, but the question of why it took such circumstances for her mother to come saddened her.

Anajah took steps towards her mother, and Denise, no longer able to restrain herself, ran and hugged her daughter.

"Mommy? Is it really you?" she said.

"It's me!" said Denise, taking a step back to admire her daughter, "I could tell that pretty face from anywhere."

The two sobbed as they clung to one another. The guards did not have it in their hearts to separate them, so they allowed Anajah and her mother to wait in the waiting area for Ms. King to arrive.

PART IV

After a hearing, and a convincing argument from Ms. King, the courts allowed Anajah to be released into the care of her mother. Anajah arrived home, more than happy to be back in familiar territory, but was sad that her grandmother was not there. The first few days, Anajah was silent, not knowing what to say to her mother. Denise often tried to make conversation, but Anajah would just answer her mother directly, not having anything further to say.

It was an early Saturday morning when Denise came into Anajah's room. "Rise and shine! I made bacon and eggs."

Anajah rolled over, not ready for her mother's high energy so early in the morning. "Okay, I'll be out in a sec."

Denise was setting the table when Anajah came out. "Looks delicious."

"Why, thank you. I am sure you can use some breakfast after staying at that despicable place. I apologize that you had to experience that."

"Me too," Anajah said, looking at her mother taking a seat at the table, with a hint of sarcasm in her tone.

Denise noticed it and continued speaking. "I'm sorry you had to experience not having me or your father around, but trust me, we would've been no good at raising you. When my dad died, your grandfather, I went to the funeral. I saw you, but your grandmother didn't think it would be wise to meet you if I wasn't sticking around, so I kept my distance; but Anajah, you must know that we both love you very much."

"My dad? Are you and my dad still together?"

"No, dear, but we're still in communication. You will meet him. He wants to meet you."

"Why couldn't you'll stay?"

"Too much history between my parents and I; you wouldn't understand."

"I understand—I understand that you two were selfish; and you two preferred your music career over me."

"I'm going to make that up to you, Anajah, I promise. I have money. I have all this I can give to you now."

"All I want is to see my grandmother. I will get ready." Anajah got up from the table, leaving her mother to stir in her guilt. Anajah's words were true, and she knew it, and they humbled Denise.

At the hospital, Anajah couldn't help feeling anxious. She had not seen her grandmother for over a month—since the day she returned from school and watched her get carried away.

"Ms. Ruth, you have visitors, may we come in?" said the nurse.

"Visitors! bring 'em in," said Ruth joyfully.

Anajah and Denise walked in. Denise puts on her glasses, squinting to make out the two individuals.

"Well, look who's back from the dead," said Ruth getting a look at her daughter, Denise.

"Hi, Mommy," Denise said sheepishly.

"Mmhmm. Hello. Is that my baby Anajah, come on over here and give your grandmother some sugar."

Anajah went running to Ruth's bedside, giving her a kiss on the forehead.

"How's Nanna's baby?"

"Good, Nanna," said Anajah, trying to hold back tears.

"And what about that crazy lady over there? How's she been treating you?"

"Good."

"Excellent. Your grandfather and I want to thank you for taking such good care of us. We honestly do not know how long we would have made it without you. You kept us young Anajah, added years to us with your youth, gave us laughter, and filled our home with love, and we are so immensely proud of the young lady you are turning out to be. He told me so himself." Ruth's own words choked her up. Emotions filled the room, bringing tears to Anajah and Denise as well.

"Let me have a word with your mother," said Ruth, looking over at Denise. Anajah left the room, leaving the two to talk. It was hard for Denise to make eye contact with her mother after many years of separation. All the years she was not there, and then to see her laid out in a hospital bed was not what she expected her encounter to be like.

"I want you to know that I'm not mad at you—and that I'm proud of the success you've made of yourself."

Humbled by her mother's words, she thanked her, with her head still lowered. "I'm sorry for leaving Anajah with you and daddy. I should have never stayed away as long as I did. Every time I thought I would come back and do right, another opportunity presented itself for me to become even greater, and I chose it instead of my family."

"Yes, your father and I were mad, but you deserved to live your life. You and that boy was not ready to raise no child. What matters is that you are here now. This is your chance to be a mother. Do not let her down; she needs you. Teach her what I wasn't able to teach you."

"What's that?"

"That money doesn't make you a success; money just makes you want to chase more money. It's your character, how you treat others, and how great you treat yourself that makes you successful."

Ruth began to gaze out the window, and Denise looked out to see what her mother was focusing on. "What is it, Momma?"

"Look, you don't see him? It's your dad, sharp as ever, just like the night we met."

"Get some rest, Mommy," said Denise, thinking her mother to be delusional.

When Denise came out of her mother's hospital room, she demanded that she speak with the doctor immediately.

71

Down the hall came Ruth's doctor, who had overheard Denise's demand. "Hello, my name is Dr. Lynn. Are you related to the patient?" she asks, taking Ruth's chart from the door.

"Yes, I'm her daughter, Denise. Are you my mother's doctor?"

"I am. She talks so much about you and her granddaughter—"

"What type of medications do you have my mother taking?" she asks, cutting Dr. Lynn off midsentence. "She's in there talking about how she sees my father."

The doctor, saddened to see another loved one losing their loved one, sympathized with her frustration and anger. "We don't have Ms. Ruth on anything but antibiotics and mild pain and fever relievers. Nothing that can cause hallucinations."

Denise calmed herself, noticing that Anajah was looking on and remembering her mother's words.

"Ms. Denise, I'm going to be honest with you. Your mother has been putting up a great fight against the pneumonia, but it is getting worse. She often says how she sees her late husband, and how he visits her. She is in her early eighties, and I am surprised she's still as strong as she is. Her body is not able to continue fighting. It may be time for you to make arrangements."

The doctor gave Denise a pat on the shoulder and walked in the room to check on Ruth.

✳ ✳ ✳

When Denise got the call from Ms. King, the child advocate had been trying all morning to get in touch with Anajah's mother without any luck. It wasn't until the eighth call that the sound of the ringing woke her up. Denise had been sleeping off an all-nighter in the studio with her artist. She took her talents into producing music, and all night in the studio turned into late mornings, still working with her artist. She and Anthony had continued to be together until she caught him in a room one night with one of his fan's years earlier. Though they still did business together, L.A. brought out another side to Anthony that Denise wanted no part of.

The news of her mother falling ill, and Anajah being placed in a shelter for young girls struck Denise. She knew, after leaving, that only sending money was not enough, but she didn't have the heart to face them after being gone for many years. Even before Anajah was born, Denise was a free spirit who was never home. The conversation with Ms. King sobered Denise, and without another thought, she fixed herself up, called her attorney, and booked the first flight headed back home.

✱ ✱ ✱

It was six am, on a breezy June morning, when Denise got the call that her mother has passed. Her body went numb, and she thought about how she had not had the proper time with her parents, and how she just left them. She thought about Anajah, and how she knew her daughter hated her for the very same reason. She got up and went to Anajah's room to tell her about the passing of her grandmother.

"Good morning. Are you sleep?" asked Denise as she knocked and slightly opened the door to Anajah's room.

"She's dead, isn't she?" Anajah's tone was hardened.

"Yes. How'd you know?"

"Just a feeling." Anajah rolled over, not wanting her mother to see her cry.

"I'm going to call family and set up arrangements. Are you going to be okay?"

Anajah shrugged. Before closing the door to Anajah's bedroom, Denise noticed the cat, made from yarn, hanging on Anajah's wall.

"Beautiful cat. I haven't seen a latch hook in some time. Did you do this?"

"No, my friend from school. My best friend," Anajah responded with her back still facing her mother.

"Would you like her to be with you during this time? We can pick her up."

Anajah turned around, tears in her eyes, and said, "Yes." She missed Naomi and wanted her company more than ever.

After the funeral, Denise had decided that it was time to have a talk with Anajah regarding living arrangements.

"So, umm, I've been trying to figure out a way to tell you this, but we're going to have to go back to where I live."

"L.A.?!"

"Yes."

"Why can't we stay here? This is where I live. Why do I have to go where you live?"

"Well, because I want us to be a family, and I'm unable to take care of you from out here. My work is stationed in L.A."

"When did you start caring about taking care of me, I can stay here and take care of myself!"

Denise put her head down, understanding how her daughter could be upset. "I know you hate me, and you have every right to—I should've never left you—but we can't stay here, Anajah. It's time for you to see something different."

Anajah began to cry. She wasn't ready to leave her home behind, her best friend Naomi, and all the memories of her grandparents that filled the home she grew up in. However, she too did not want to be without her mother, so off to L.A. they went.

DANCING IN DARKNESS

DANCING IN DARKNESS

—————⟶꩜⟵—————

2016

"You don't care about me, or what I like. You just care about being right," said Delores as she talked to her friend, Mansah. She was wiping down the tables, preparing to leave for the day.

"That's not true. I just know more than you, so I try to be of great service."

"Oh please. Every Friday night, you come in here thinking you're dropping jewels, when all you are looking for is a great conversation with me."

"That may be so, seeing as how your conversation is something I do look forward to."

Mansah handed Delores a tip. "Here's a little something," he said, then he waved goodbye to her and the owner, Mr. Carmichael, who was standing behind the counter, closing out the register.

"That was the last customer. Let us go lock up now so we can get home in time," Mr. Carmichael said, bringing the register to the back. Delores was now wiping down the counter when Mr. Carmichael came from the back with his hat, signifying that it was time to go.

"One of these days, you're going to have to let me take you home," he said, giving her food he made for her and her mother.

"No, that's okay. You know I like to walk."

"Okay, suit yourself, but be careful, there's a lot of creeps out there. Say hello to your mother for me, will yah?"

"I'll be fine, and I will."

Delores gave Mr. Carmichael a hug, and then the two went their separate ways. Walking down the Vegas strip was one of Delores's favorite things to do. From all the people, tall buildings, lights, and casinos, there was always some form of hustle and bustle taking place, making her feel that she was not alone. The further Delores walked away from the strip, the quieter the blocks became. She came to a dark tunnel, with puddles of water and rubble laid in front, with the outer layer of the tunnel's walls covered in graffiti. When most people would turn away from such a dark place, not Delores. She walked with her head high, unafraid of the darkness that laid ahead of her. For she lived in it, born into it.

✱ ✱ ✱

In June of 2000, Delores was born to a streetwalker named Laura in an alley not too far from the Vegas strip where she currently resides. She was raised on the streets, and due to Laura's lifestyle and choices, they were forced to live out of Laura's car. Delores learned survival skills at an early age, but her lessons came with much pain. Her mother would leave her with random people so she could go make her money and being exposed to such a lifestyle affected Delores in more ways than one.

To entertain Delores, Laura would read her books she would take from the library. One of the very first books Delores learned how to read on her own was "Are You My Mother?" by P. D. Eastman. Noticing her love for reading, Laura began getting Delores chapter books to keep her busy; by the time she was nine, she had completely read "Roll of Thunder, Hear My Cry" by Mildred D. Taylor, one of the first times Delores felt a sense of achievement.

It was in the middle of the night around this same time when Delores and Laura lay sound asleep when two men came banging on their car window with crowbars, waking them.

"Stop it, get away!" shouted her mother, while Delores went under her covers and hid in the back seat of their van.

The men were also homeless drug addicts that stayed under the bridge nearby. The crowbar smashed the window, and one of the men went straight for the radio and searched the glove compartment to see what else he could find that was of value, while the other was fixated on Laura and began tugging and pulling at her. The other guy, still searching the car, noticed Delores, but pretended he didn't, knowing his partner to be a menace.

"Come on, let's get out of here," he said, trying to pull his partner away from Laura, but his partner would not let up. Laura fought back, kicking the man as hard as she could, giving her time to run, leading the men away from Delores, who was still hiding in the back seat. When she peeked her head up and saw the men chasing her mother, a rage began to overtake Delores. She got out the car and picked up the crowbar dropped by one of the men, and tucked her switchblade given to her for protection in her jean pocket and followed them.

Laura was tackled to the ground, and the man began tugging at her jeans. The other man ran off, not wishing to add accessory to rape to his list of crimes for the night. With her daughter out of sight, Laura laid there, leaving *her body, and taking her mind elsewhere—a coping mechanism she learned throughout the years. Delores crept up slowly, eyes focused, ready, and willing to do whatever was necessary.*

She came up behind the man on top of her mother, and quietly reached for her blade, before he could see what was coming, Delores' knife was lodged in the back of his neck. Since that night, Laura was sure to find another place to live for her and her child, seeing that living out of their car proved to be too dangerous. She found a group of people, living in abandoned tunnels who accepted her and her daughter, allowing them to live amongst them, and Delores and Laura have been down there ever since.

Though they lived underground, the mayor of the tunnel made sure Laura and Delores had everything needed: a kitchen consisting of a hot plate and pots and pans donated by outreach workers; a personal bathroom the people living amongst them help them make, which had buckets that held water either from rain or bottled water; and tents for their bedrooms. How the mayor was able to help them connect to electricity was a mystery to Delores and her mother, but being so grateful, they did not care to find out. Many people would be afraid of living in such a place on their own, but Delores and her mother were protected and accepted by the people amongst them.

As time passed, Laura's addiction got the better of her, causing a stroke, which resulted in her being numb from the waist down. In a way, Delores thought the stroke would stop her mother from using. She refused to purchase drugs for her mother but gave up when watching her mother detox cold turkey proved to be more painful than she thought. She did not know what to do, and by this time, Delores was now fifteen years old. With her mother sick, and having no one to depend on, Delores was left to make difficult choices.

* * *

2016 CONTINUED...

Delores had been working at Mr. Carmichael's diner for almost a year. They met when she walked in hungry, and by the look of things, he knew that she was in trouble. Normally, a person with the appearance of Delores would not be allowed in his restaurant. Her face was smudged with dirt, and clothes were unkempt, but he saw something different in her. She explained to Mr. Carmichael that she hadn't eaten in days and would work for food. He brought her to the back, fed her, and allowed her to wash dishes for the first few weeks.

Mr. Carmichael told his wife about Delores, and she did not hesitate to donate clothes and other hygiene products to the young girl. He gave her a job as a waitress, noticing that she cleaned up nice—and would often cook for Delores and her mother. He did not pry, seeing that Delores was private, and she only spoke of her mother. He was happy to help in any way he could.

"You're later than usual, what yah bring me?" asked Laura, knitting in her wheelchair.

"Mr. Carmichael's special of the day."

Delores handed her mother her food.

"Great, now where's the rest of it?" asked Laura, taking the sandwich.

"Mommy, I'm going to get you some more, just give me time."

Laura looked at her daughter, trying to refrain from lashing out. She was running out of her drugs, and not having any choice but to wait on her daughter was driving her mad.

"Mansah came by to see me," said Delores, hoping to change the topic.

"Him again? You two are getting close."

"Yeah, he just needs someone to talk to."

"Does he know where you live?"

"Nope. Come on, Mom, you know he'll look at me like I'm some type of freak."

"Okay, okay, when you're ready, he can get you outta here. Start a different life…"

As they spoke, the mayor came rolling down the tunnel; he was too in a wheelchair. "How's everything over here? Y'all good?"

"We're okay. How about you?" asked Laura.

"Not so good. There has been a killing in one of the tunnels. On the other side, but still, it's too close. So, be careful."

"Oh, wow! Any word on who did it?" asked Delores.

"No, no one even recognizes the victim. I don't know what's going on around here anymore. So, we must look out for one another."

The mayor rolls away, leaving Delores and her mother to ponder over what he said.

"Don't worry, Mom. I will keep you safe."

"I know." Said Laura remembering how Delores protected her when she was younger.

Delores went into her tent to get ready for bed. As she undressed, she noticed her switchblade was not in the same pocket she had put it in before she left for work. She took it out and noticed blood on it. *The last time I remember blood being on this thing, I was nine*, she thought to herself. She cleaned it off and got ready for bed, putting the mysterious blood on her knife towards the back of her mind and focused her attention on getting her mother's heroine.

ISABEL

Isabel was on the prowl. She needed at least four johns for the night to be good for the week. She worked out of a motel on the back streets of the Las Vegas strip.

"Where you been, Isabel?" said Cherry, a twenty-year-old girl she met while working on the stroll, and her connect.

"We're in Vegas, where haven't I been."

"Girl, I know that's right; I see you got that look in your eye. How many you need?"

"Four, got some things I need to take care of. Hey, I need some more of that stuff too."

"I'll let my guy know."

"Thanks."

The two girls continued their night. The last customer of the night came in a black car when Isabel was getting ready to leave.

"What's your name sexy?" he asked, rolling down the window and pulling up aside her.

"They call me Isabel. What you need, baby?" she said, with her head in the window of the driver's car.

"Get in."

Isabel got into the john's car, assuming it was Cherry's friend with the drugs, and they drove off.

"So, do you have it?"

"You in a rush or something?"

"No, just want to make sure I'm the right girl for you. That's all."

Isabel became quiet. Something inside her knew she was in trouble by the way he was speaking. *I should have just kept walking; I already had my four,* she thought to herself.

"I've been watching you, stay to yourself, quiet. Let me fix you up, make you some real money."

"I don't want a pimp," said Isabel adamantly.

"Well, it really isn't what you want at this point. Like I said, I have been watching you. Be my girl, and let's make some real money." He handed her his card and four hundred dollars. "Meet me at this address tomorrow evening." Then he stopped the car to let her out.

"Shit. A problem I didn't need." She said out loud, watching the car drive off. She saw Cherry running towards her. "Hey, my guy is on the way. Thought you was about to leave without it. Everything okay?" Cherry asked, seeing the fear in Isabel's face.

"Yeah, I'm okay," said Isabel, not wanting to mix Cherry up with what she had going on. Isabel headed home after getting what she needed, and while walking, she thought long and hard on how she was going to get out of her situation.

✻ ✻ ✻

Delores woke up, groggier than usual; her head was pounding, and her feet ached. She grabbed her flashlight and headed to the bathroom to wash up, where she noticed a black bag stuffed in the corner.

"Hey, Mom, what's this black garbage in the corner of the bathroom?" asked Delores, giving a light knock on her mother's tent.

"I don't know, baby. You must've put that there when you came home last night," said Laura, peeking out her tent to see what Delores was talking about.

Last night? I did not go out last night, Delores thought to herself. She looked at the clock sitting on an old dresser between the two tents and saw that she was late for work. "Mama, I gotta head out now, work my shift."

"Hold on, Delores. I need to talk to you about all this work you're doing."

Delores entered her mother's tent and noticed a needle.

"Come on, Mama, put that away, I know you do it, but I don't want to see it."

"We all have our vices. Now, where did you get all this money? This all can't be coming from the diner," she said, holding up a stack of cash. "Where did you get that from?"

"From you, Dee. What's going on with yah?"

"I don't remember giving you that, Mama."

Delores' mother takes a second and looks at her daughter. "You threw it in my tent, along with my stuff after coming out the bathroom, and then you went inside your tent."

Delores looked at her mother and took the money, counting it. "I don't remember."

"Well, it's here now. What should we do with it?" asked Laura, dismissing the details of how it appeared.

"Let's get a motel or a room, Mama. We have enough to set us up."

Delores' mother smiled at her daughter. "Nah baby, I like being away from people. You go rent a room—go ahead and get your life in order. Mine has already been lived."

Delores looked at her mother, confused. "What are you saying? We still have a chance at a normal life, and plus, I cannot leave you down here. That's not happening. Now, put all your paraphernalia away, eat, and I'll be home later with dinner." Delores blew her mother a kiss, zipped her tent up, and continued getting ready for work at the diner.

When she walked in, Mr. Carmichael noticed her appearance and brought her to the back. "Is everything okay, Delores?"

"What do you mean?"

"Take a look at yourself in the mirror, honey."

Delores ran to the bathroom and saw her face covered in smeared makeup. *When did I have all this makeup on?* She washed her face and fixed herself. Then she walked out of the bathroom to face her boss. "Guess I missed a few spots, I apologize."

"No worries, everything alright?"

"Yes. Just got a lot going on, taking care of my mother and everything, but everything's good."

"Okay, but if you need anything, you know you can tell me, right?"

"Of course, but you do enough, allowing me to work here, and the food. I couldn't ask for more." Delores thought about telling her boss of the situation she and her mother was in, but after being quiet about it all her life, she didn't think to bother others with her circumstances. She had learned to accept it and went through lengths to hide it. As her shift was nearing its end, Mansah came into the diner. "Let me walk you home," he said.

"What's with everyone wanting to take me home?"

"Someone, please walk this young lady home," said Mr. Carmichael, closing the register.

"No, no, no, I'm fine," Delores said, dashing for the door.

"Have a great night and say hello to your mother for me."

Delores waved and headed out before anyone of them would pressure her into taking her home. A few blocks away, she remembered that she had forgotten her and her mother's food. *They should be gone by now,* she thought and headed back to the diner. She pulled out her keys and saw that Mr. Carmichael had left her food wrapped up on a counter, with a note saying: "I knew you would be back." Delores smiled.

As she was about to walk out, she noticed Mansah across the street sitting in a black car talking to a guy. She waited so that he would not see her. She watched the man he was talking to and could not help but feel like she met him before. He looked sketchy to Delores; the pair did not match. The gentlemen in the car reminded Delores of the man that would come and see her mother when Delores was younger. They finally drove off, and Delores headed home, unable to shake the feeling of Mansah and the sketchy fellow.

When Delores got home, her mother was up, waiting for her.

"What's this?" she asked, holding up a mini skirt and crop top.

"Clothes."

"Don't get smart with me. It's only me and you here, and I haven't been able to fit clothes like these in years."

"Maybe one of your friends from down the tunnel brought it over. I don't know, Mommy, but it's not mine. I keep my clothes in my tent."

"Listen, Delores, you're sixteen, and you have your whole life. You do not want to end up like me. The money's quick, but the streets will eat you up even quicker."

"Mom, I know." She handed her mother her food and went into her tent. Something was going on with Delores, and she did not know what. She could not understand where her mother got that money from earlier, and she didn't understand the makeup or the clothes. She understood why her mother would think that and that all clues pointed to her, but she could not remember. She began searching through her things and came across a card with the name Adonis written on it, along with a location, time, and date.

"That's tonight!" Delores got herself ready and headed out to the address on the card. She came to a motel and knocked on the door, and to Delores's surprise, it was the same man who was talking with Mansah from earlier.

"Hey, I found a card with this address and the name Adonis on it."

"Come in."

"Oh, no, that's okay, I just was trying to figure out something. Do you remember me or remember giving me this card?" she asked.

"You're kidding me, right? We had this conversation the other night. Now come in."

"No, I have to get back, I just wanted to—"

"I wasn't asking you."

Behind the man, Delores could see other women, and she reluctantly entered the room and took a seat on the edge of the bed, away from the others who all pretended to be busy.

The man closed the door and looked at Delores. "You do seem different, Isabel, cleaned up a bit. But I hope you don't think faking amnesia is going to get you out of working for me."

"Oh, I'm afraid you got the wrong girl. My name isn't Isabel, and I already have a job."

"Well, I'm the one who gave you that card, and I gave it to you while you were working them back blocks."

As Delores tried getting her thoughts together, out came Mansah from the bathroom.

"Mansah?" said Delores, noticing him. "What are you doing here?"

"Same reason you're here, to make some real money. I have been watching you; I admire how you keep your day job and work at night. A real go-getter who keeps to herself. I had to tell Adonis about you."

"You set me up?" asked Delores.

"Well, I wouldn't quite put it like that. I saw a pretty girl who wasn't making any real money working at a diner and wanted to help, so I told my homie about you."

Delores began rocking back and forth as Mansah continued.

"But imagine my surprise when my homie told me that he saw you out by the motel—and that you were going by the name of Isabel. You can't tell me it isn't fate."

"I'm not a prostitute, and my name isn't Isabel," said Delores, still rocking with her head lowered.

"Look, whatever, Delores, Isabel—whatever you want your name to be, it'll be. But you officially work for me now," said Adonis.

Delores got up and stumbled a bit, trying to catch her balance as she went for the door.

"No, no, no, you're not leaving until we have our personal party," said Mansah.

He grabbed Delores, bringing her onto the bed. Adonis left the motel, bringing the girls who watched along in silence with him, leaving Mansah and Delores alone.

"Please, Mansah, you have me confused. Please don't do this."

Ignoring Delores, Mansah continued to force himself onto her. Noticing that she stopped struggling, he paused and looked at her. She was checked out, unresponsive, and gazing off into the ceiling. He stopped and gave her a light smack across the face. "Delores?" she slowly blinked, and responds,

"I am not Delores." She let out a loud laugh, an obnoxious laugh that even startled Mansah.

He jumped off and moved back, noticing that this was not the same girl he was visiting in the diner. This girl was not meek like Delores. She possessed a more aggressive spirit. Slowly, he called out to her by the other name, "Isabel?"

"I am not Isabel, either, though I know both. I even know you. Could not understand what Delores saw in you. She actually liked you, and this is what you do."

Mansah looked at Delores, confused. "So, if you're not Delores, and you're not Isabel, then who are you?"

"Why don't you come back over here and find out, or are you scared?"

Mansah accepted the challenge, climbed back on the bed, and got on top of Delores. When he was not looking, out came her switchblade, and into his ear it went. She pushed him off, grabbed her stuff, and said to the body that was once Mansah, "My name is Desiree."

VEGAS, BABY!

Anajah was happy to be on vacation. Her work had driven her to the point of insanity, and she and her best friend, Naomi, decided to take a trip together to Las Vegas.

"You know Drake will be performing tonight."

"Stop it!"

"Yes, girl, and we must get backstage. You know he has a thing for cougars," said Naomi, giving Anajah a wink.

Anajah laughed. "I'm sure with the way we're going to behave, no one is going to expect us to be adults. It's been such a long time since I let my hair down," said Anajah.

"Feel yah. Although you did have more fun than any of us once you moved to L.A."

"Yeah, you can thank my party-crazed mom for that."

"How is she?"

"She's great now. Went through a bit of a dark spell, but she's back on track."

"Good. Let us get these bags into our rooms, and get some alcohol inside of us, immediately… Vegas, baby!" said Naomi.

The two women laughed and talked about everything they wanted to do as they waited for their Lyft to take them to their suite at the MGM Grand.

DESIREE

Delores ran home, with the Desiree personality still in control. Though Delores was not aware that she created other personalities, her other personalities knew of her, and everything about her. She ran home, face drenched in sweat, hoping that Adonis was not chasing her. She made it to her tunnel, and while walking through, she was stopped by a stranger looking to score meth.

"Wrong tunnel," she said.

"Well, what can you give me?"

"I don't have any drugs. Please leave me alone."

The stranger, relentless, started walking alongside Desiree, making conversation. "How old are you?"

Desiree ignored his questions and slowed to catch her breath.

"You look far too innocent to be traveling in such a dark place alone."

When she continued to ignore him, the stranger became forceful, grabbing her arm and dropping his bottle of liquor to get her to stop walking.

Desiree looked at the intoxicated stranger. "Sir, I'm having a rough night. I would advise you to get off me before you end up like the other gentlemen who tried this a week ago."

The stranger laughed, showing all his rotting and missing teeth. "Or what, little girl? It ain't every day I come across a pretty little thing like yourself."

"You won't let go of my arm?"

The stranger, still grinning, was now trying to press his smelly body up against Desiree. She pushed him off, and he pulled a knife on her. "Listen, this can go the easy way, or the hard way," he said, making up in his mind that he was going to have his way.

Desiree stopped fighting back, giving him the impression that she was surrendering so he would not see what was coming next. She pulled out the same switchblade she had just used, and into his gut the knife went. He backed up, looking at the blade in his stomach. She screamed and charged him, pulling the knife out and stabbing him repeatedly until he was no more. Her cries turned into laughter as she staggered away, disappearing into the darkness of the tunnel.

She made it to her living space and noticed her mother still in her wheelchair sleeping. She hurried into the bathroom and washed herself using the water bucket that was heated by a portable stove. Then she put all her clothes in a black bag and stuffed it behind the buckets. Knowing no one would be able to find her, eased her. Desiree was born the night she saved her mother, and Isabel came about once her mother was confined to a wheelchair.

Delores was not brave enough to accept the fact that she would have to give her body up to take care of herself and her mother, let alone her mother's drug habit. The thought of having to do such a thing traumatized her, along with unfortunate things that happened to her when she was younger, left alone with strangers.

The warm water from the rag eased Desiree, allowing Delores to come back. She stood in the bathroom, trying to remember what she was getting ready to do. She peeked out the curtain and noticed the time and realized that she more than likely came from work and was getting ready for bed. She noticed the black bag again behind the bucket; and decided to open it, and what she found took her by surprise: bloody clothes and more provocative clothing and makeup.

"What the—Mama, what is all this?" she said, coming out of the bathroom and noticing her mother asleep in her wheelchair.

"Mama come, let me put you in your tent," she said, turning her wheelchair around, but what she found she was not ready for. Her mother was slumped over, eyes rolled in the back of her head with a needle stuck in her arm. The sight made Delores daze off, and she began to cry hysterically, dropping to her knees. "Please, Momma, wake up. Don't leave me. I do not know how to live without you. Please, wake up, Mommy. Please, you are my only friend."

Delores helplessly cried, lying at the feet of her mother, trying to process what she was seeing. As she lay there in tears, glimpses of her night begin to fill her head: the murders she committed, Mansah and his true intentions, and Adonis, the man that she was now hiding from. She ran into her tent and curled into a ball, hoping that her night was nothing but a terrible dream. That is when everything started making sense to Delores—the clothes behind the bucket, the extra money, the knife having blood on it. It all made sense, and Delores thought herself to be a freak. She left her tent, crying on her hands and knees, crawling to her mother's lifeless body still in the wheelchair.

She was able to gather herself and went into her mother's tent, collecting all things that were close to her, including pictures of her parents and a bracelet her mother had given her. She put the bracelet on her mother's swollen wrist. Then she grabbed the bag from behind the bucket, covered her mother, and rolled her out of the tunnel and into the empty lot covered in gravel. There, she encountered the dead body of the man who had tried assaulting her.

She positioned her mother's wheelchair beside the body and took the unfinished bottle of alcohol the stranger had. Delores poured it on top of her mother and guzzled the rest of it. And with her mother's lighter, she set her on fire, throwing the black bag containing her secrets into the flames.

"You're free now, Mommy." Delores looked at the body her other personality had killed a few hours earlier, poured what was left in the bottle on the John Doe, and set that body on fire as well. She sat on the gravel and watched the flames engulf them, getting rid of memories that once were.

Delores turned away from the fire, gazing into the Vegas lights in the distance, filled with grief, anger, and confusion as to who she was. Her body dragged itself, as she began walking, staggering off to the light that lay ahead. She came across a statute that looked to have three heads and began speaking to it.

"Why me? What could I have possibly done that was so wrong that I was given such a life?" Not too far from the dazed and intoxicated Delores was Anajah and Naomi. "One of your patients followed you to Vegas?" said Naomi, nudging at Anajah to get her to notice Delores.

"Woah, what happened to this young girl?" said Anajah, noticing Delores.

"No, Anajah, I see that look in your eyes. We are here on vacation."

Ignoring her friend, Anajah walked over to Delores. "Hey, are you okay? What's your name?" Delores looked over at Anajah, but said nothing, and turned away, now staring at the traffic going by. Anajah continued, "How old are you? Where do you live? I can call someone," said Anajah, now pleading with Delores. Delores continued to ignore Anajah and began walking away from her.

Naomi cautiously walked up to Anajah. "Something's not right with her, Anajah; we should leave her alone."

Anajah continued watching Delores as she walked away and noticed that she was not slowing down as she was nearing oncoming traffic.

"Why isn't she stopping?" asked Naomi.

Anajah ran and grabbed Delores, pulling her back before she walked into traffic, and Delores collapsed into Anajah's arms.

✳ ✳ ✳

Delores woke up in the hospital, IV in her arm, trying to remember how she got there. The nurse walked into the room.

"Hey, how did I get here?" she asked.

"Your aunts bought in," said the nurse.

"My aunts?"

"Yes, one of them is still here. Want me to bring her in?"

"Please," said Delores.

Anajah walked into the room. Delores stared at her, trying to remember how she knew this woman.

"Hi," said Anajah as she waved at Delores. "My name is Anajah."

"Hi Anajah, where did you find me?"

"You were about to walk into the street."

Tears began flowing down her face when memories of seeing her mother dead and the events of the night resurfaced. "Why didn't you let me?" Delores asked sobbing.

"I couldn't do that. I'm sure there's too many people that love you and want you to live." Said Anajah now consoling her.

"I have no one."

"Don't cry—tell me your name." Anajah gave Delores tissue from her bag to wipe her face.

Delores refused to speak, not knowing if she could trust Anajah.

"I'm a clinical psychologist. I can help you, but you have to let me know who you are, and your age."

Delores took a second and decided to speak. "I think I have many names, but right now I'm Delores. I'm sixteen, and I have no one."

Compassion overcame Anajah as she got a better look at the young girl she had saved and from hearing the overwhelming sadness that came out with every word she spoke. Delores's age did not match her weight, for she was small, and her deep brown eyes had become swollen from crying. Her hair was wild, and her skin and lips were dry, and her face and body were badly marked up.

"I'm going to get you some food and some clothes. Is there anything else I can get you?"

"A book, please."

Anajah pulled out a book from her purse. "*Secrets from The Ruler* by Vonda Violet," she said, handing it to Delores. "I'll be back, Delores."

Delores was already immersed in the book and did not hear Anajah, who walked into the hallway and called Naomi. "I'm thinking I can help her," she said to Naomi when she answered.

"How did I know you was going to say that? Anajah, what happens in Vegas stays in Vegas. Have you not heard that expression? It applies for everything in Vegas, even for psychotic teens."

"Blah blah—let me know when you're done at the spa."

Anajah hung up the phone and called her mother, telling her of the young girl she had met and asking her opinion of what she should do.

"Don't leave her, Anajah. It would not sit well in your heart, trust me. If she wants to come back with you, bring her." Though Anajah agreed with her mother, she knew her mother's response was an emotional one due to the choices she made, and Anajah realized that her wanting to save Delores may be backed by personal reasons as well.

Delores was released from the hospital, and Anajah brought her back to her suite. Delores thought to run off but knew she had nowhere to go, and Adonis was looking for her. Delores looked around the luxurious hotel. Though she had been inside before, it was only to see what she could find, but never to stay as a guest.

"Okay, this is us," said Anajah as they got off the elevator and began walking to their suite. When Anajah opened the door, she continued speaking to Delores, explaining that she could take her room and everything she had planned for them to do, but Delores could not hear her. She was too busy checking out the décor of the room, for she had never seen anything like it. The ceiling windows in the living room area gave her a captivating sight of the Vegas skyline. Anajah noticed Delores taking it all in and let her be.

Naomi came through the door with bags and take out in her hand. "Girl! Please tell me you are going out tonight because I invited that masseuse over and… oh, hello," she said, noticing Delores on the couch, who was still staring out the window. Delores looked at Naomi, gave her a smile, and continued her gaze.

Naomi smiled and ran to Anajah's room. "Umm, so, what are you doing?"

"Look, Naomi, she's going to stay in my room. Don't worry; we are still going to have a great time—"

"Anajah, you can't help everyone. What do you even know about this girl?"

"I know all that I need to know."

"And what exactly is that?

"That she needs help."

Anajah left the room to check on Delores, not wanting to hear anything that went contrary to what she felt was the right thing to do. "Are you hungry?" she asked.

Delores shook her head. "I don't have an appetite."

"What food do you like to eat? You must eat something." Anajah handed Delores the menu.

"What happened to your parents?"

Normally, Delores would shut down when asked so many questions, but she was overwhelmed with hiding and continued to open.

"I never met my dad, and my mother is dead."

"I'm sorry to hear that, Delores," Anajah said, feeling bad for asking.

"Why did you help me?" Delores asked curiously.

Anajah took a second before answering. "Because I would want someone to help me."

Naomi came into the living room, feeling guilty about her initial reaction when seeing Delores on the couch. "Anajah, leave the girl be. How about we all do some shopping and enjoy the rest of this vacation?"

"Yeah, that does sound like fun. How about it, Delores?" asked Anajah.

Knowing that she had a pimp in search of her, Delores knew she could not go back outside. "How about if I stay here and finish reading the book you lent me at the hospital? That would be great."

"Okay, you can order whatever you want—charge it to the room—and if you get tired, you can take my bedroom," said Anajah, pointing to her room.

"But where will you sleep?"

"Naomi's room, the couch, doesn't matter. Here is my number; call me if you need me, or if you need anything. I'll come right away."

Delores took the paper with Anajah's number on it and thanked her. Anajah and Naomi left, giving Delores time alone.

Waiting until they were on the elevator, Naomi began to once again question Anajah on what she was doing. "Anajah, I know that you're an expert in this field and that I'm only a middle school teacher, but I promise you, there is something wrong with that girl."

"That may be so, which is why she's in the right hands."

"You need a cape; make sure we pick one up," said Naomi, making Anajah laugh. "But seriously, you know you should've called the cops."

"So, she could be held, and then put into some institution. No. I could understand if I weren't professionally trained, but I am."

"Okay, girl. You know I got your back, even when I think you're wrong."

✳ ✳ ✳

The door closed, and Delores broke down in tears. This was the first time she ever been in a place so beautiful, and she wished her mother could have been alive to see it. She got up from the couch and began looking around, noticing the marble island and cloth chairs surrounding it, as well as the cherry wood walls and golden décor. Delores went into the bedroom that Anajah told her it was okay to go in. The bed, so plush, so beautiful—the soft carpet on the floor, the closet—everything a girl could dream of. She looked over and noticed the bathroom and went inside. She saw herself in the mirror and understood why Anajah was so concerned for her. Her face was dry, lips cracked, and had dark circles that surrounded her eyes.

The only time Delores took showers was when she turned into Isabel, and would spend evenings in the motel, which was almost every other night. Other than that, her usual way of washing was out of buckets filled with rain, and bottled water kept warm by an electric stove. Delores turned on the shower and undressed. She got in and allowed the water to run from the top of her braids on down. The hot water and steam filled the room, and Delores fell in love with the water, and she washed as if it was her first time, disappearing into the steam.

✳ ✳ ✳

Anajah and Naomi did not return to their suite until minutes before the sun came up. They managed to open their room door, laughing, and falling all over each other, still intoxicated from bar hopping after a day of shopping. They went into the kitchen in search of water to sober themselves up.

"Hey, hey, hey, where's the princess?" said Anajah as she headed to her room, remembering Delores. Anajah opened her bedroom door and saw Delores, wrapped in the hotel robe, under the covers, and sound asleep.

"Aww, look how cute she looks. I remember when I was sixteen. So young, with my whole life ahead of me," said Naomi.

"Okay, let us get you to your room. You need to rest." Anajah helped Naomi to her room before passing out on the couch herself.

Anajah woke up after only three hours with the sun beating down on her. Delores was sitting on the kitchen island staring at her, startling Anajah. "Uhhh, good morning. Delores, you okay?"

"Yes, I was up and didn't know what to do."

"Oh, okay. Hope we didn't leave you alone for too long?"

"No, I was asleep most of the time."

"What did you order?"

"I don't have an appetite."

"Still? We must get you eating, young lady. Here, we got you some clothes," Anajah said as she went to the bags she and Naomi had left at the door when they came in. She handed most of them to Delores. "These are for you. If they are too big or too small, I kept the receipt in the bag for exchanges."

Delores looked at the bags and took them slowly. "You bought all of this for me?"

"Yeah, we saw some things we thought would look cute on you. Plus, we wanted to get you something before I went back to L.A., and before Naomi went back to New York.

"You two don't live out here?" said Delores looking disappointed.

"No," said Anajah, noticing the sadness overtaking her. "But we're not leaving until tomorrow, so we still have time to hang out."

Delores remained quiet, not sure what she should say or how she should feel.

After a short pause, Anajah said, "How about this? You try on your new clothes, I will make some breakfast, and we can discuss what we will do today, and what you will do once I leave. How does that sound?"

Delores agreed, and not too long after, Naomi emerged from her room begging for coffee, giving Anajah and Delores the first laugh of the morning. The three of them enjoyed breakfast as they planned their day. Excited about what was on the itinerary, Delores could not help but be a part of it.

The ladies had a great day at the spa, laughing and talking like they were sisters who had grown with each other for years. They got massages, meditated in the saunas, and got their nails done. Anajah had not seen mood nail polish before and ironically chose that, fascinated by how it changed color when it was underwater. Pink to gray… Delores loved it; she loved everything about the day, for it was the first time she felt she had true sisters, and it was the first time she had ever been pampered in such a way. The love Anajah and Naomi gave her made her want to live. She realized there was much she had not experienced, and feelings that she hadn't explored.

Naomi was off flirting with a fellow from London, while Anajah and Delores sat near the fountain in the middle of the lobby, enjoying their sorbet. Delores was still enamored by her nails.

"You really like them, huh?" asked Anajah.

"I do."

"I don't get it, Delores, a beautiful, kindhearted girl like you—where's your family, where have you been staying?"

"I think I have an appetite now," she said, changing the topic.

Anajah sighed. "You are like the little sister I never had."

Delores smiled and then she heard a man's voice calling her name. Her heart stopped until she realized it was just Mr. Carmichael.

"Delores, I can hardly believe that's you. You hit the lotto and forgot about me?" he said, admiring her new appearance.

Delores smiled, thanking him for the compliment, but seeing him started bringing about weird feelings, and Delores began to breathe heavy, and Anajah noticed the sudden change in Delores.

"Hello, my name is Anajah, Delores's friend," said Anajah, sticking out her hand, giving Delores a minute to get herself together.

"Well, I had no idea Delores had such marvelous friends. Where has she been hiding you?"

Anajah laughed. "That doesn't matter. I'm here now."

Mr. Carmichael laughed and brought his attention back to Delores. "Can I have a word with you, Delores?"

Delores and Mr. Carmichael took a few steps away from Anajah to speak in private. Mr. Carmichael explained that there was a man who had come by looking for her and that she should lay low for a while and not come by the restaurant. Delores thanked him for telling her and knew it was Adonis.

"Enjoy the town, ladies, and Anajah, please take care of her. She is a sweet young lady. Say hello to your mother." Mr. Carmichael waved goodbye and went about his business, happy to see that Delores was in good hands.

*** * ***

Seeing a shift in Delores' demeanor, Anajah told Naomi that she was going to take Delores back to the room. When they got back, Anajah observed Delores. She could tell she was in deep thought, and Anajah wanted to help. "Delores, let me ask you something. Do you have sudden dramatic shifts in the way you perceive things, think, or feel?"

Delores looked at Anajah, thinking about the question before answering. "Yes."

"Do you ever try and understand why your mood shifts the way it does?"

"I mean, I guess it's just the way I am."

"I couldn't help but overhear that he told you to tell your mother hello; I thought she passed away?"

"She did, Anajah. I would not lie to you. He just doesn't know it; it happened just the other night. The night you found me."

"Oh my, Delores!" Anajah began comforting Delores.

Delores opened about her mother being an addict, and how they lived on the street, and in tunnels. All Anajah's training and previous patients had not prepared her for Delores. Her heart melted thinking of a young girl, alone with her mother, her only friend, surviving on the street; Delores even told Anajah about the pimp who was forcing her to work for him, but she didn't mention that she had taken life before.

"You're coming with me. A pimp wants to what... Oh no!" Anajah remembered her composure and relaxed for the sake of not rattling Delores.

"If you are okay with it, Delores, I would like for you to come back with me. You do not need to bring anything, just yourself. Do you want to come back with me?

Delores thought about it and wanted to say no, for she had not told Anajah everything and felt that it wouldn't be fair. But she also knew that to stay would mean her death or being Adonis' slave, ending up like her mother. "Yes. I want to go with you."

***

When they got to the bus station, Anajah and Naomi hugged each other, almost in tears that they had to say goodbye.

"See you next summer, bestie, and welcome to the sisterhood," said Naomi as she hugged Delores then headed to the airport to catch her flight.

As Anajah and Delores waited for their bus to arrive, guilt began taking over Delores. "Anajah, I can't go with you."

Anajah looked at Delores. "After what you told me, I'm not leaving you here."

"But I think I've killed."

"Delores, how does someone think they've killed? They either know, or they don't."

"I know, but I have blackouts, and I can't always remember what happens when I do, but I know I have before."

Anajah stared at Delores, knowing that Delores admitting she has committed a crime meant a huge risk, but it was a risk Anajah was willing to take. "We'll discuss more of that when we get home. But only when we get home and are alone."

Delores was surprised at how well Anajah took such news and was happy that she found someone she could be open with. Although Anajah knew it was risky taking a teenager who's experienced such trauma, she knew from personal and professional experience what can happen to teenagers who did not handle such trauma properly, and something inside her couldn't turn her back on Delores. A strange part of her felt as if the whole purpose for her coming to Vegas was to save her.

BEFORE THE STORY

———————— ᦔᖇᦔᖇ ————————

The Queens lay on the grass, looking on as the sun began to set.

"What do you think the Ruler's new planet will be like?" asked Queen Jeannie.

"From what I hear, it sounds similar to the Kingdom," responded Queen Nilah.

"Well, I hope it turns out better than Venus. I can't understand why the Ruler allowed it to get so bad," said another queen, Queen Onaka.

"Come on, you know that wasn't the Ruler's fault. I've heard talks about how Sono turned that place into a complete disaster," said Queen Nilah.

"I just hope we're strong enough to get through our assignments. The royals who've returned from Venus explained that the challenges are nothing like they imagined," explained Queen Jeanie.

As the queens continued to ponder as to what was to come, their royal mates came, carrying fruit and laughing amongst themselves.

"Would we be disturbing if we join?" asked King Melchez, Queen Nilah's husband, handing her a fresh cut piece of mango.

The Queens looked up and noticed their kings. They all moved, making room for them to join.

"Not at all," they said.

✲ ✲ ✲

Before Earth had a dream, and Queen Onaka took on her assignment and became Emily, Queen Jeannie as Vonda, Queen Nilah as Anajah, Queen

Leena as Naomi and Princess Noni as Delores—they lived amongst each other. As we can see, the assignments that the queens (and soon we will discover, the kings as well) have taken on have proven to be challenging. But what a peaceful time they shared, laying amongst the wildflowers, in a green field, in the kingdom, under the lilac sky.